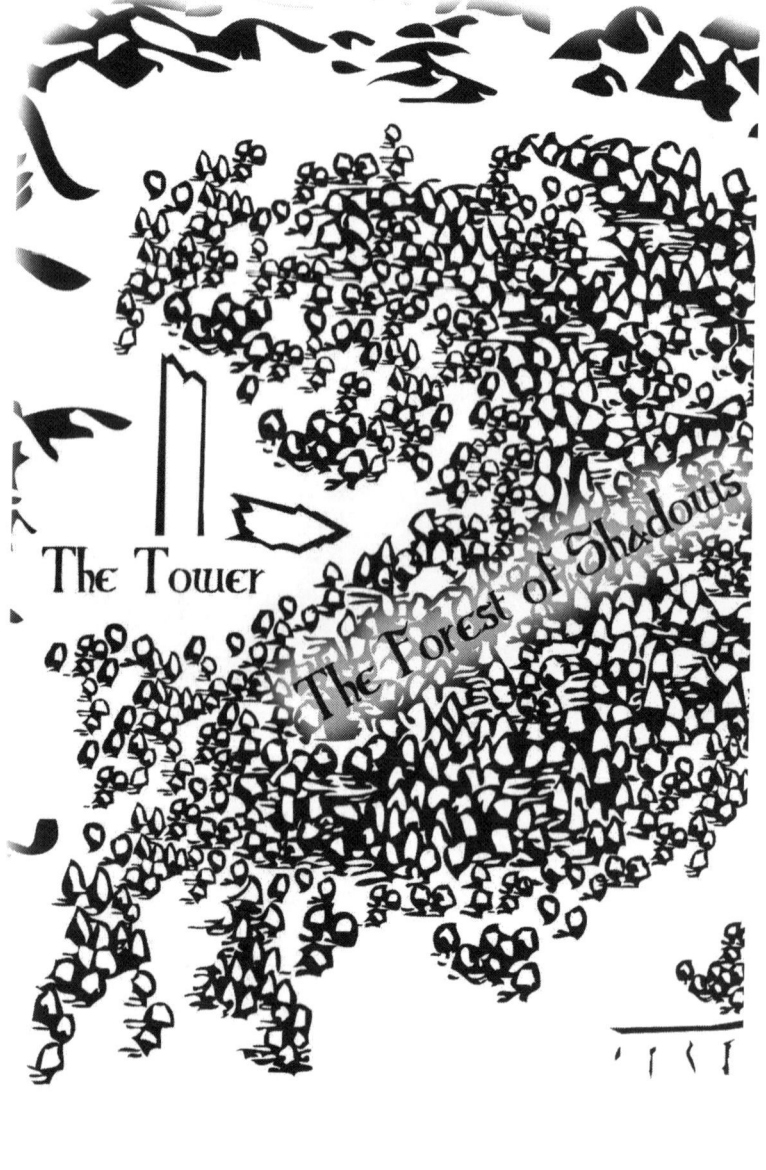

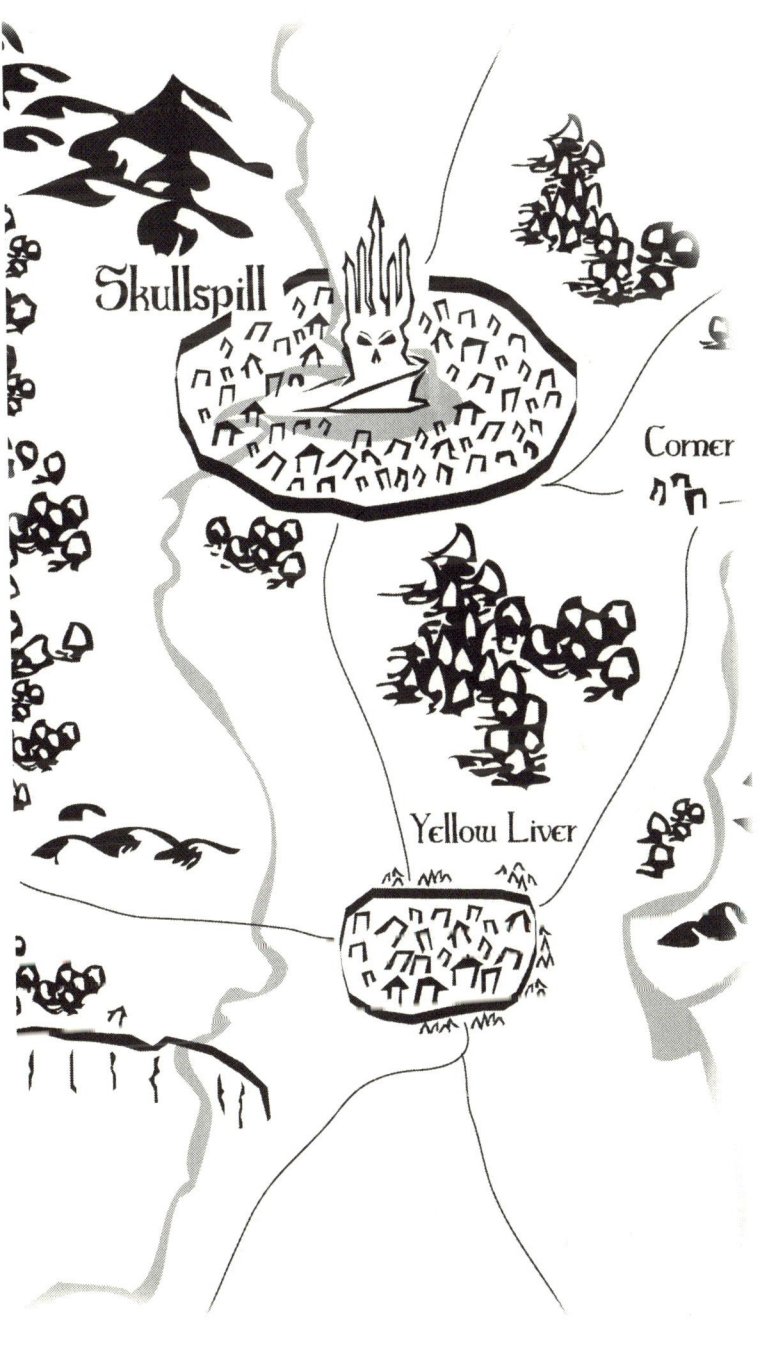

The Saga Of Ukumog

Wracked
Desecrated

WRACKED

By Louis Puster III

*Sean,
Thanks for making sure no one walked off with my sword at AnnoCon 2014.
Best wishes,
Louis Puster III*

This is a work of fiction. All the characters and events portrayed in this book are either products of the author's imagination or are used fictitiously.

WRACKED

Copyright © 2012 by Louis Puster III

All rights reserved, including the right to reproduce this book, or portions thereof, in any form.

Edited by Morgan A. McLaughlin McFarland
Cover Art by Chandler Kennedy
Maps by Louis Puster III

Second Edition
ISBN 1478123133
ISBN 978-1478123132

First Edition: January 2010

For Jen, Jesse, and Mom

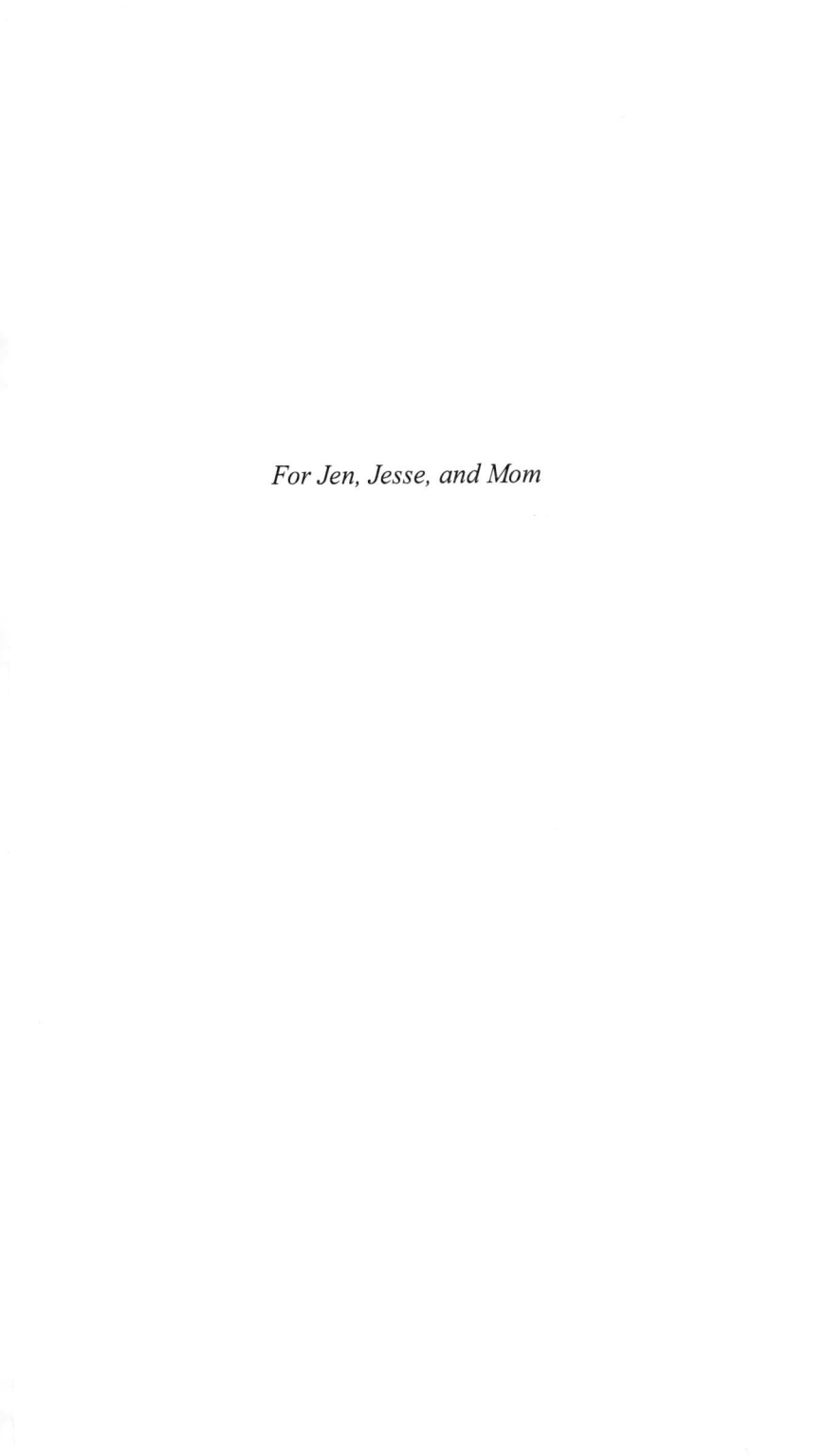

Acknowledgements

There are a few people who have helped me give flesh to the world of Wrack and Ukumog, and I would like to thank them here:

To Amy, Colin, Chris, Jorge, Kat, Mark, Patrick, Roger, Ryan, Scotty, and Zane for the first forays into the world.

To Brandon, Golden, Kristen, Leslie, and Maynard for that short and deadly romp in the woods.

And Blaine, Brian B, Brian P, Jesse, Pat, Rob, Robin, and Sean for braving the monster it became afterwards.

Stories can be told in many ways, with many people contributing, and this one is better for the marks you all left upon it.

Finally, to my parents and grandparents. You nurtured my imagination and encouraged me to tell my stories. The simple fact that you listened and smiled was the greatest gift. Thank you.

Chapter 1

Red. My vision was nothing but a flat and featureless plane of red. Before the simple comfort of my monochromatic world color could fade, darkness and light entered my vision in the form of shadows and highlights. Black soon joined the original red. Forms appeared slowly as if emerging from a bloody fog. The dark shapes appeared first, as if they were claiming the light that possessed the space they lusted after. Slowly the dark places became sharper and formed an image that I could grasp.

The face I saw was streaked with deep wrinkles that spoke of darkness and hatred, yet his eyes showed a balance of intelligence and purpose. His black hair, smoothed back over his head, erupted into curls near his shoulders. Dark and piercing, his commanding gaze was heightened by the nearly feral look on his face. A short and pointed beard came off his chin like the tip of an obsidian dagger.

As I pulled back from the intense face and my view widened, I could take in more of the man who stared directly into my soul. His shoulders, which had previously been blurry, became clearer. The macabre pauldrons that rested on his shoulders were gore-encrusted and aged; nonetheless, I could make out the pile of skulls, twisted together by a mass of worming and grasping tentacles.

Wracked

Again, my vision expanded and more of the man became clear. The rest of his armor was similarly covered in images of tentacles violating and gripping the skeletal remains. Pulled tightly over his torso was a tabard as black as the void, trimmed in red. His right hand gripped a blade that was also covered in viscous blood that dripped to the surface below. The ground itself was not just simply earth; this commanding man stood upon a pile of bodies in all states of life, death, and dismemberment.

Surrounding the man was an army of armored men wearing the same blank tabard. This calm moment of examination was enhanced by the fact that they were all moving impossibly slowly. Before them was a crowd of unarmed, apprehensive children and adults. Without warning, the army exploded into action like a machine of war and death. Their blades whirled as they ground their way through helpless opponents, leaving a trail of death and gore behind them. The unarmed innocents became overwhelmed with fear and could do nothing to escape their bloody doom. In the eye of this storm of metal and blood, the commander's expression plainly said the violence fed something deep inside him.

I had been dismissing the muffled and distorted sounds I heard as mere noise, but an unmistakable scream of pain carried from somewhere far away to my ears. At that moment, there was a flash and I was no longer transfixed by the carnage that had encompassed my entire world.

A black tower loomed over a forest growing at the foot of a mountain range. The thick and ancient trees were completely dwarfed by the massive tower. Above the tower, a sky full of rapidly changing clouds scudded across the horizon. The sun and moon streaked across the heavens. The speed of their travel increased

Chapter 1

until the light was balanced between night and day in a perpetual twilight. Another piercing scream violated my mind and again there was a flash.

I was back to the commander and his grinding murder machine. Helplessly I watched, as more of the innocent were gutted in a gruesome ballet. A driving lust for blood and death was obvious in the commander's gleeful smile. Suddenly he snapped out of basking in the massacre that surrounded him. His expression became neutral and his gaze turned directly toward me. I saw a focused concentration appear in his eyes, his baleful stare looking right through me. Fear crept into my reddened world, and the horror of the scene that surrounded me hooked into my heart. All I wanted to do was escape the commander's powerful stare. A scream came from somewhere close by, and I turned to see who it could have been. Before I could find its source, there was a flash and the scene changed again.

The black tower was again the focus of the new image, but the tower seemed frozen in time, and the top half had been severed from the rest of the tower. The displaced upper half now lay silently on the ground not far from the tower's base.

Another flash, and more colors entered the world. A pair of green eyes filled my entire view. I saw in them pain and disappointment, and they held me in thrall. I saw the spark of life start to leave them just as another scream hit my ears. This scream sounded broken and horrid, as though it came from a throat that had not made a sound in years.

Wracked

My eyelids peeled back and my eyes met complete darkness. My mind reached out to my body, and even the thought of moving sent a shock of pain through my system. The smell of damp, musty earth surrounded me. I panicked and lashed out with my arms and legs, like a helpless bug trying to escape from its cocoon. The mossy blanket of earth that covered me tore away and light flooded into the dark pit that now gave birth to me. The light seared my eyes, and burning protest from my joints surged through me as a crackling scream. Even the sound of my own voice was alien. My bones ground against each other like ancient millstones, and my scream changed into a choking cough which flung dirt, muck, and bugs from my throat.

After the sharpest of the pain had left me, I sat and recovered my strength a bit, distracting my mind with the bugs; they, too, had been evicted from their rest and needed a moment to adjust to their new surroundings. The intensity of the light attacking my vision slowly faded and my sight became much clearer. Breathing became easier as I evacuated small, chunky streams of black earth from my throat. Moments after the coughing stopped, I felt more aware and, like the bugs at my side, I also began to take in my surroundings.

I had crawled from a grave near the roots of a dead, or dying, tree that might once have been tall and strong, but had become gnarled before finally succumbing. The tree stood on a low hill near a pool of water fed by a small waterfall. The top of the waterfall's cliff was also covered in twisted trees.

After surveying the area and finding nothing familiar, I studied myself. A tattered and weathered black robe covered me. The robe's many-layered cloth was frayed and worn, yet entirely dark as pitch. Around my waist was a woven belt of black and red cord, with tiny silver skulls hanging around the knotted ends. It was then that I saw my bony and pale hands. Deathly pale bluish-

Chapter 1

white skin was stretched taut over them, the nails dirty, yet glossy. Without thinking, I put them to my face, and was unsurprised at how cold and hard they were. My fingers' exploration of my face revealed nothing unusual, as far as faces go, yet I was compelled to see my face for myself. Ignoring the shooting pain that came as I stood, I lumbered towards the pool of water that lay a short distance from the falls. Walking was harder than I expected; I stumbled a few times on my way to the water, and the pain forbade me from trying to stand again. My need to see the secrets of my own image spurred me on, and in my anger I found strength to pull myself through the muck to the edge of the black pool that was fed by the falls. The dark water, thick with decaying plants, was eerily calm where I met it.

The face that looked back at me was like a stranger's: deathly pale like my hands, but with a hint of strawberry blond hair on the top of my head and on my chin. That bit of color gave me a glimmer of hope that there was some life still left in this walking corpse. The blue eyes staring back at me looked as if they might once have been bright, but were now stormy and piercing. The dark grey flesh that surrounded those eyes truly made me look like some sort of messenger of the dead. The black pallor also stained my lips like a pestilent cloud of death. "What am I?" I asked no one in particular.

For what seemed like eternity I lay there on the bank staring at this unknown person who found his way into my life. My mind was a blur with countless questions about who I was, even the very nature of my existence. I had no answers. I could only search the few moments I had been awake and the images that had been my companion in the tomb. Without thinking, I touched the surface of the water and shattered my reflection. The trance the pool had over me broke, and my thoughts turned to answers. What greater purpose lay behind my awakening and the dream itself? Curiosity caused a courage to grow in me and I pulled away from the rippling mirror that showed me a dark stranger.

Standing posed a painful problem that took me some time to solve. The answer seemed to be in the struggle, as each pulse of pain made me stronger. More than once I fell to the ground. Each time I looked over at the pool and saw the ripples from the falls marching in waves over the surface of the water. My desire to find answers found pace with those waves and drove me on. After much dogged effort I was triumphant, and I took further stock of my possessions. I found black leather cords bound around each of my wrists, with such knots that no amount of wrestling would undo them. Whatever I had been tied to, my bonds had broken, but the leathery shackles remained. Around my neck was a similar leather cord that had likewise been tightly tied. A tiny black chain—hanging around my neck, but hidden in my robe—held a simple iron key. The key, as unknown to me as my own purpose, I tucked back into my robe. I went back to the hole from which I had escaped to see if anything else lay hidden within, but I found only black moss and dirt.

The light in the sky had begun to fade. With no desire to remain where I had been entombed, I picked a direction and began to walk. As I left that dark and twisted glen, I heard no sound of creature or other person, as though time and the world had forgotten it was even there. For a moment I wondered if the world had likewise forgotten me.

If you walk in a particular direction long enough, you can't help but find a path or road. When I came to one, I simply followed it. The grinding pain in my muscles and joints faded with time and movement. When the pain was little more than a whisper

Chapter 1

on the wind, I believe I started sleepwalking. Floating somewhere between my earthly struggle and the misty visions in my head, I was barely aware of my surroundings.

I must have passed other people on the road, though I only recall vague flashes of dull color. I remember some stares, and I remember ignoring them, as I did not know how to respond. Hours and miles passed away in a dreamy haze. Whatever I had become, I was not encumbered by the needs of the living people. I felt no hunger, and my body was tireless. The mist in my mind receded, and I saw light gradually fill the sky. On the horizon I could make out a black scar with dark clouds looming over it. It beckoned me, a call I could not help but answer.

Sometime later I felt living energy teeming around me, and saw that I neared a walled city. The gate was guarded by a few men taking tolls and checking wagons. A cloud of people wandered around the area, many of them waiting to pass through the gate. Others were asking for food or money. Some had given up on any hope of entry and created their own hovels against the high stone wall. It was this vitality that I felt all around me that was beckoning me. It flowed into me and awakened me from my sleepwalking haze.

By the time I came to the gate itself, my desire to enter the city burned within me. I was so focused on getting inside that I barely heard the guard speaking to me.

"Oi. 'ou deef?" He said with words so broken I could barely understand him.

I looked up at him uncomprehending, aware only that he had spoken.

"Tax to enter is six pennies," said the more charming of the two dirty, burly men.

Wracked

Their faces were obscured by tarnished and beaten helmets, and I could glean nothing from their scarred armor and black tabards. I starred at them awkwardly; I had nothing to give them, but all I could think of was entering the city. My gaze was fixed on the bustle beyond the threshold of the gate. After a few moments of silence, the more eloquent one spoke.

"Right, if you don't have the tax, you can't go in. Move aside."

Looking past them I hesitated, still hypnotized by the life within. My mouth filled with a sweet flavor at the anticipation of entry.

The rougher of the two broke my longing with a harsh shout, "Oi! Move aside!"

My desire broken, I stumbled backwards. Defeated, I found myself walking away from the line and joining the rabble of begging rejects. They clawed at me and pulled me into the crowd of them. They tugged, groped, and searched me for valuables. Finding that I had none, their desperate hands quickly shoved and pushed me further towards the back of their crowd, until finally I was on the other side of them. I got some strange pleasure in being washed by their hunger for life. When their search was over and they discarded me, I felt strangely sated.

Once through the beggars, I found myself amidst the hopeless and sickly living within the hovels. Dizzy from the movement around me, it took me some time to settle into the hurried activity of life. I found a place to sit near a hovel with no door, and focused on the people surrounding me. In the center of the hovel, a person bundled in cloth coughed uncontrollably every once in a while. I could not help but be drawn into watching the figure, though I could not tell whether it was a man or woman.

Chapter 1

After sitting there for some time, children living in the filthy honeycomb of huts emerged slowly. Undoubtedly, they were driven by curiosity to see my gaunt shape and empty gaze. One brave boy came and sat by me, staring at my face. At first I tried to ignore the children, but the brave one reached forward and touched my exposed hand. He recoiled from the cold, hard flesh his fingers encountered. The other children fled in a mixture of joy, shock, and fear at his reaction. Not the boy, though; he kept staring at me with those dark eyes. They shone with a wonder that must have been reflected to the surrounding world in my own stormy eyes.

Time passed into evening slowly. I could nearly count the time ticking by the coughs coming from the open hut near me. The boy stayed near me and even after his desire to stare at me faded, he played with the rocks and dust that surrounded us. At dusk there was commotion by the gate. I heard weapons drawn and a woman's strong voice yelling. Whatever was the cause of the disturbance, life went back to the normal hum of begging and movement almost as quickly as it had been disturbed. The steady sound of the people at the gate reminded me of the waterfall that had greeted me after I escaped my grave.

As soon as the light faded, the gates closed and the guards disappeared into the dark city beyond. The beggars left, and fires were lit up and down the length of the wall. The residents of the hovels cooked whatever filth, vermin, or actual food they had found during the day. The various smells of their cooking collided into a pungent mess of odors that was slightly offensive, even to my dulled senses. I watched them eat like the pack of scavengers their situation had made them, and they ignored me. It was at this feast time that my young companion left me, undoubtedly to fill the empty pit of his belly. I was not hungry, yet I understood the painful emptiness they sought to fill. The simple devouring of flesh would

Wracked

not sate my hunger; this hunger burned somewhere other than the pit of my stomach, yet, it was kept at bay in a way that I did not yet understand.

While the darkness of night blanketed everyone, there were those who could not rest. Both the sick and the cunning fought for survival. The quiet that came with the night was comforting. Those who were not sleeping avoided my gaze and gave me a wide berth. As before, most did not even acknowledge that I was there. An outcast amidst outcasts; somehow this was not unfamiliar.

Staring at what stars I could see through the clouds and haze of the night, I contemplated my situation. There seemed no answer to my identity or how I had ended up in the grave that birthed me. Odd, too, was the fact that none of the people I had seen were horrified by my deathly appearance. Perhaps the sick and the desperate had worse things to fear than monsters such as me? A burst of action interrupted my meditation, but from where I was sitting, it was impossible for me to see what happened at first. I saw a few people getting knocked around, as if some of them had gotten into a fight. Earlier, there had been a few minor disagreements over food or some such, so I expected that things had just escalated. When I heard the screams and wailing, I knew I was wrong.

People scattered. Some of them rushed to the gate and began banging on it in a vain attempt to find shelter inside the city. There was no response from within the walls to any of the commotion. The boy who had sat with me for a time ran toward me. Compelled by his obvious fear, I stood up. Instinctively the boy ran behind my rotted robe. I scanned for what he was fleeing.

"What's going on?" I asked, with a calculated purpose that surprised me.

Chapter 1

The boy said nothing, but raised a pointing finger at something lurking atop the pile of broken wagons that he called home. I saw them: hunched figures with long and strong arms, clutching children in their claws. I could not see how many beasts there were. Their movements were quick and brutal as they leapt through the crowd, grabbing several of the children and a few of the slow-moving adults. The hands of the boy clutched my robes so tightly I could feel him shaking with fear. This boy, who just a few hours ago was braver than any other person here, was filled with terror. I wanted to help him, to free him of that terror, but how? I had no weapon and no knowledge of those creatures. I did the only thing that came to mind.

"Hey!" My voice pierced the noise, and for a second everyone and everything stopped and looked at me. The creatures let loose a sickening noise, something between a gurgle and a hiss, and leapt over the walls and into the night. There was a brief silence, finally broken by the cries of mothers who had lost children and the moaning of the wounded.

Turning to face the boy, I said, "What were those things?"

It took him a moment to respond. "I dunno. Some of the old people say they are ghouls or ghasts or somethin'. I dunno what they really are."

"This happened before?"

"Yeah. They used to come only once in a while. But now, it seems like someone goes missin' every night."

The fear had left his eyes, and I could see the courage and curiosity coming back.

Without lifting his face to me, he asked, "Are you dead?"

The way he blurted the question made me smile. It was so awkward, yet genuine, that I could not reward him with silence.

Wracked

"Do you think I am?" I asked, hoping he might answer some of my own questions.

"Nah. Dead people don't walk around, and undead things can't think."

The shock and sadness of the little shanty village surrounded us, yet the boy seemed unaffected. This life of hunger, sickness, and nightly attacks had made these horrors common for him. I wanted to ask him his name, but I knew I could not respond in kind, so I did not ask. We sat there examining each other for a short while. When he did get up to head home, I realized that there were no parents waiting for him. Had he lost his family in the one of these nightly attacks?

By the time that light returned to the sky, I was convinced that the secrets of both my identity and the attacks could be found within the city. My resolve to enter the city strengthened. As much as I admired the brave boy, I doubted that shouting would drive the creatures away a second time.

I spent the next day studying the activity near the gate and waiting for the right opportunity to slip past the guards. There was nothing I could sell to make the coin I needed to get in, and the guards were just confiscating the money of those who were obviously begging at the gate. After hours of assessment, I decided to seek another entrance. The creaking in my bones was not as bad or painful as the day before, and the mist in my mind had all but burned away. Eventually, I found another gate. This one was smaller than the other and only had one guard. As I approached, I saw a crowd gathered and heard raised voices.

A woman with thick black hair was yelling ferociously at the guard. He did not seem amused. Occasionally he shouted a word back to her, but the fight was definitely hers, and it seemed that soon it might come to blows. I positioned myself to sneak

Chapter 1

past the guard if a fight did begin. It seemed the argument was not about how she didn't have the money to enter, but that she didn't think she should have to pay. The guard let out a disgusted noise to dismiss her. Before he could react, she landed a mighty blow upon his face which caused him to fall backward into the muck. She pounced on him and punched him in the face again and again with the viciousness of someone who doesn't fight for the fun of it. With no other guard in sight, I saw my chance and slipped past the commotion. While I slid into the city, I saw her look up at me. There seemed to be a tiny glimmer of a smile on one side of her yelling face, but she quickly turned her attention back to the guard. Seconds later, the gate was far behind me and the bustle of the city had absorbed my presence.

The city's inside seemed no better than its outside. Filth and refuse littered the streets, and the people who wandered within their disgusting tax-bought reward were no prettier. The sounds of coughing and retching floated over the smoky corridors of stench and garbage. The stones of the street had been stained black by the decades of sickness that had been trampled into them by the greasy people. While the clothes of the inhabitants herein were finer than those of the beggars outside, they were covered in the dirt and stains of hard labor and hot summers. The sights and smells were uncomfortable, but that was nothing compared to the noise. Carts banged loudly against the uneven black stones of the street, People screamed and shouted just to talk, and those selling their wares were twice as loud. All of my senses were assaulted by this irreverent and unpleasant cacophony of misery. There was no joy in the eyes of any person that I could see. In fact, just my looking caused a mood shift for the worse in most people. Why would the city go to such lengths to keep people out? My naiveté about the city guard would soon be at its end.

Wracked

Later that night, I found a less disgusting part of the city. With my hood up to hide my condition, I skulked around in alleyways. The people who I encountered on the fringes of the city that I found behind, beside, or even under the buildings were not helpful. I asked the folk that I found in those cracks between society about my condition and the attacks outside the walls. Their answers seemed to indicate that the people in the city had no idea that attacks were going on, and no one even seemed bothered by my unusual appearance. There was no brotherhood between the people on the fringe, however, and my lurking would not remain a secret. Late in the night two guards accosted me, one with a battered face that I recognized.

"Oi. We 'eer dat your askin lotsa questions. Wot's your name, filth?" The taller, unwounded guard asked me.

My failure to respond only spurred them on. The one with a swollen face reached out a hand and pulled away my tattered hood.

A smile revealed blood stained teeth. "Yup. Dis is da one I saw sneekin' by when dat woman was distractin' me."

I laughed at his lie.

"You got somfing to say?" The battered one asked, aggressively.

"From what I saw, she was beating your eyes into the back of your skull," I should not have replied.

"Wut!" His swollen eyes got as big as they could, and he threatened me with a fist.

"Easy, Larry. Dis one has a mowf on 'im. Let's see wot else he knows."

"Right. Cap will pay big fer a King's man. You're a King's man, ain't cha?" Larry of the swollen face asked.

"What King?" I asked, confused.

Chapter 1

"Joker, eh? You see wot we does wif jokers." The sinister tone in the tall one's voice was hardly necessary; a knife glinted in his hand.

Raising my empty hands to them defensively I said, "I have nothing to give you, if that is what you are looking for."

The two men laughed. "Wot, no gems hiddin' in dat grave you climb'd owt of?" Larry's voice was sarcastic and cruel. I knew then that it was only violence they wanted.

Lust for blood overcame their desire to toy with me. Rolling my body to either side to evade their blows, I suddenly recalled being in many fights. A flood of violent memories filled my head like a flame, distracting me long enough for the tall one to plant his knife in my belly. The pain rippled through me. This was different than the other memories – it had a rush with it, like an old friend I hadn't seen in years. This friend was not happy to see me, or I him.

The knife entered my chest, belly, shoulder, and neck repeatedly. Each time a ripple tore through me and a swelling numbness filled the void in their wake. I heard the two men muttering that they liked how long it was taking me to fall over and give up, right before everything went dark.

Floating in a stone room, I found myself staring at a beautifully detailed mural, made of precious gemstones. The image depicted a giant circle of huge draconic figures all grasping each other's tails with their teeth. Each was of a different color, save two who glistened with the colors of all the rest mixed together. Fascinated by the most trivial details, I found myself unable to see the whole picture, even with effort. My vision was turned away from the mural by some unknown force and I took in the remainder of the room. I realized that the mural was in fact the chamber's ceiling. Now I saw the utter vastness of the chamber beneath me. The walls were draped in light-absorbing velvet curtains that seemed too large for anyone to have actually made them. The glimmer of gold and silver and the heavy smell of incense assaulted my senses. Muttering and muffled noises told me that I was not alone. Below me was a small host of dark figures. Of them I could discern no details at all. I only knew that they went about their business as if I did not exist. Blearily, I watched them wander about the room, listened to the blurred noises they made, and found myself confused about how clear the room was in comparison. When I tried to call out to them, I found myself abruptly somewhere else.

The green eyes that had previously shown disappointment filled my view. This time they were laughing, and they belonged to a handsome and charming man. As his movements slowed, I studied every nuance of his laughing face. It was lined with years of joy and bright with unyielding hope. From the faces of others sitting with us, I knew that he had just said something outrageously funny.

We were in a pub of some kind. I looked into my empty mug and realized that the only sound I heard was the laughter of the crowd. The charming man seemed to ask me a question, and pointed to his mug as he stood up from his seat. Concern wrinkled his handsome face, and the world began to sway and suddenly went sideways. Stunned, I did not even try to stand. I felt his hands shake me. His mouth opened to a roar, but I still only heard the laughing crowd. His eyes hovered over me. His mouth moved as he stared into my eyes.

"Are you alright?" said a woman's voice that seemed to come from the charming man's mouth.

Chapter 1

His eyes faded and I found myself staring into a different pair of green eyes. A woman's green eyes.

Wracked

Chapter 2

"You alright?" she asked in the same voice I heard in the dream. The eyes and voice were part of the same violent woman who had facilitated my entrance to the city.

Stunned for a moment, I paused before responding. "I think so," I said, as I tried to stand.

As she pulled me off the ground she remarked, "You are lucky I happened by and was in a generous mood. I had to kill one of them to get them to stop." With one quick and fluid motion she spun her blade through the air, shedding the lingering blood from its edge, and then gracefully slid it into the sheath at her hip. For the second time she issued a smile at me with a warmth that seemed uncharacteristic for the tiny bit I knew about her. "Some people just can't resist the temptation of being cruel."

Speechless, I drank in the dark contradiction of this woman, how coldly and matter-of-factly she had just talked about taking life. I looked over to one side and saw the limp body of the tall one thrown to the side like a discarded doll. The worn grey stones which made the surface of the street were slowly growing crimson borders outward from his body.

"Let's get you out of the street. That other one might come back."

Wracked

Following her lead into the street, I looked at the empty faces of the people around. I decided that hiding myself might be prudent, so I pulled the tattered cloth attached to my robe, that might at some time previous been a hood, over my head and face. I tried to subtly find the lethal wounds I knew I should have on my torso, only to find holes in my robe and pale unblemished skin below. Confused, I continued to follow my dark haired savior to our unknown destination.

Tall, skinny buildings pressed together on narrow streets, adding to the confusing and oppressive feeling of this labyrinth city. I gave up counting the spots in corners or shadows that I could sit in should I want to ambush some passerby. She led on, never seeming to even question which direction to go. Once she even tossed me back a gentle smile that again was contradictory to her harsh demeanor. Still, this kindness that came from her, no matter the reason, was not something I could ever remember. Unlike the moments of flashing memories, there was nothing that told me I had ever been treated this way. The void of my soul consumed her kindness and wanted more.

"Here we are," she stated as she walked towards steps of a place called *The Headless Mermaid*. It had begun to rain enough to drive most people indoors. The rain stirred the scent of the streets into a rancid stink. I was eager to get away from both the cold rain and its smelly companion. We shoved our way through the wet host of people all trying to find shelter, warmth, and a drink to get inside.

Inside was a crowd just as ugly, loud, and horrible as one you would expect to find in a place with this name. With a hard stare, the raven-haired woman disarmed a rough looking group of their table and motioned for me to sit down. Her hand made a drinking motion as she disappeared in to the dirty crowd. A little

Chapter 2

laugh boiled up from inside me at the lust mixed with fear that much of the crowd had dripping from their eyes as she passed. Something tugged at my side.

Next to me stood a very short man who had a gnarled face, and wore a black cloth skullcap. The look in his eyes was one of someone who had spent his life looking for something, and had finally found it. My eyes were drawn down to a medallion around his neck. It was a black circle with silvery tentacles escaping from its edges. In the center of the circle, a pair of white featureless eyes seemed to glow with some sort of hatred.

"Yor him, ain't cha," the hopeful man asked. "Tha one dems call Wrack." He removed his cap in some awkward gesture of respect, then looked over at the crowd. My eyes followed his gaze to find the woman returning with two mugs. When I looked back, the little gnarled man was gone.

She slid me one of the mugs and sat in a chair across the table from me. I could hear the creaking of leather and clinking grey scales of her armor even over the noisy room. I caught her trying to follow my eyes into the crowd in my vain attempt to find the little man. That strangely warm smile floated to the surface of her face when our eyes reconnected. We sat in an awkward silence in the middle of a hurricane of drunken commotion. Eventually she broke it.

"What did you do to those guards? Had to be something to get them to stab you like that."

"I sneaked into the city during one of their watches. At least I think it was one of them. Whole thing seemed a little random to me."

Wracked

"Oh, yeah. I saw you sneaking in while I was pummeling that one guard. So probably revenge, then. Hrm. Seems like a pretty harsh penalty for just skipping the uzkin' toll." She uttered that curse like a professional.

"Ah. I thought that was you. Maybe I should pay you the toll." I laughed uncomfortably.

"Maybe you should." She said with a straight face and a tilt of her head. Then she smiled and gave a tiny laugh.

Again the silence between us grew, both of us sipping on a horribly thick and bitter brew. As horrible as it was, it tasted better than the black earth I had coughed up what seemed like a lifetime ago. Looking into the black liquid in my mug, I got lost for too long thinking again of how I had found myself in that hole. When I came back to my senses, she was speaking to me again.

"Brin. My name is Brin. Honestly, I'm not in the business of saving strangers from what was probably coming to them. Guess that means you owe me more than just a toll." The coldness with which she spoke seemed to almost flatter her it was so natural. She paused to drink. "So, lets have it. What's your name?"

Knowing that this moment would come, I should have been more prepared. No knowing what to say, I responded with the first thing that came to my mind. "Wrack."

"Like the torture machine, the rack?"

"I suppose. Never thought about the meaning before. Just a name really."

She looked at me suspiciously for a moment. "You tainted folk are always so strange. Never met one of you that hasn't had a weird name."

"Can't honestly say I know what is strange and what isn't. Around three days ago I—"

Chapter 2

The front door of the tavern opened. The wind and rain outside had grown more intense, and with this large portal open into the tavern the wind came rushing in. It brought a wet and sharp cold that made every person in the place turn and curse the fool—a tall and lanky fellow, covered in a drenched cloak—who had let in the unwelcome guest. It turned out that this fool was Brin's friend, which became obvious when she laughed at him and then beckoned him to join our small table.

"Avar! Where in the sundered gate have you been?"

Our new companion removed his soaked cloak to reveal a boyish looking man with blond hair and a bright and charming face. If that didn't make him stand out enough, he was wearing shiny pauldrons attached to an armored mantle, both covered in silvery runes. The craftsmanship alone seemed to be out of place with his otherwise patchwork armor and clothing. He flashed a winning smile at us before sitting down.

"Sorry, Brin. Got held up at the gate. Did you know that there are hundreds of people who can't even get into the city? They have no right to deny people the ability to see their families or try and find work. They are all out there living in putrid shacks; it's horrible." His gaze drifted over to me, then quickly back to Brin, as if he had just seen something that he refused to acknowledge. Brin found this very amusing.

"Avar, this is Wrack. I saved him from being stabbed by the guards today. See? I told you that I can do good things once in a while."

He continued to look at her, and while I couldn't see his face, I imagined a look saying, "Are you kidding? There is no way I am talking to that freak."

"Rack? Like a thing for spices?"

"Perhaps."

Wracked

"Odd name. Glad to meet you anyway. I am Avar." He greeted me genuinely and warmly. I found myself surprised by his friendly demeanor. "As Brin probably told you I am a Shad—OW!"

Brin's violent movement and the fact that her fork was now missing made it rather obvious that she had just done something vicious to Avar's leg under the table to stop him from talking. Part of me was grateful for that interruption. I knew I had no context to talk about whatever topic Avar was going to bring up. I preferred that my new friends had secrets. It made me feel like we were on the same level, even if I didn't know what my secrets were.

"Seems I helped Wrack here get through the gates by beating on one of the guards this morning, only to save his life from a pair of guards tonight. How's that for coincidence?"

Avar's face changed to one of complete fascination. "I keep telling you, Brin. There is no such thing. There is a greater plan tha—OW! That really hurts!"

This time his yelp caused a few heads to turn and look at our table. Drawing attention like that obviously made Brin unhappy. She leaned over and whispered in Avar's ear and he nodded, after he rubbed the sore spot on his knee.

"Sorry. Avar isn't used to being in dangerous places. Has a tendency to ramble on about things he shouldn't in places he probably doesn't belong in the first place. I am trying to teach him to be a little more city-wise without him having to get in as many fights as I did."

"I think I have been in a few fights in my time, too," I said, my voice full of uncertainty, "but I honestly don't know."

Chapter 2

Avar wasn't really paying attention; he was busily assessing his leg for damage. The look on Brin's face was one of curiosity and suspicion. After another gulp of the horrid brew she cleared her throat. "You don't know how many fights you have been in?"

"No. I seem to have misplaced my memory."

"How far back can you remember?"

"Only a few days. Really nothing before I—"

"Before you what?"

I saw judgment lingering on the edges of Brin's eyes. I felt a dark resentment rising within me, direct at either Brin or at my strange distance from the world around me; I am uncertain. Swallowing the darkness, I tried to answer her. "Before I crawled out of the ground."

Avar looked at me with eyes wide. He shifted in his seat as if he were preparing to either fight or run. Brin continued to give me a steely look, waiting for me to say the wrong thing.

"Avar, what is the difference between the tainted and the animated again?"

His voice cracked as he spoke, "Uh. The animated are corpses that are puppets to the will of a greater force. The tainted are still living people who have been touched by the power death and trapped into a seemingly dead or dying body. But, they are usually tied to one of the Doomed."

"You sure?" She asked without taking her eyes off of me.

"Uh. Yeah."

With slitted eyes Brin asked, "Which one of the Doomed are you the slave of?"

Quickly I rifled through my limited memory, trying to find the right answer to her question. The word Doomed had no meaning to me. So, I answered as honestly as I could, "Doomed? I don't know anyone named Doomed. If I was, as Avar said, tied to one - they must not like me very much. Since I woke up alone in a grave."

I was certain that they both were about to draw their weapons and cut me to ribbons. That same dark sickness within me even wanted them to. My face did nothing to betray the struggle within me to the outside world. I sat there silently, waiting for their judgment.

Brin sighed, "I just saved your life. I am not about to take it just because you might be some horrible corpse creation. Besides, you certainly don't act like any servant of the Doomed I have ever seen."

Complete confusion took over Avar's face for a moment, but then the realization that he wouldn't have to fight let him ease into the idea of not killing me. "I hope you're right, Brin. Last thing we need is one of the Doomed after us. So, how did you save our new friend anyway?"

"I had to kill a guard."

"Uzk. We are screwed. Enjoy the meal, Wrack. Last one we are going to have."

I appreciated his sentiment, even though I had no food. Just the bitter brew, and it was tasting and smelling worse as it warmed.

"Calm down, Avar. I killed three guards when we fled from Bile. We will be fine."

"If you say so. I don't think you can keep acting like this without consequence."

Avar was more correct than he realized. As we sat in the Headless Mermaid more than just a storm was brewing outside.

Chapter 2

After a few hours of chatting in the main room of the tavern, Brin invited me to stay with her and Avar. I helped the drunken Avar up the stairs as we headed to their room. "I like you Wrack. You seem like a good person. For a dead tainted guy, that is." Brin just rolled her eyes at Avar's drunken ramblings. She produced a key when we neared a door a short way from the top of the stairs.

Once inside the small room, I saw that there were only two beds, one on either side of the room. with a window in the wall between them. "This one is for me, and that one is for Avar. I am afraid the floor is the only place not spoken for."

"The floor will be fine."

Avar kept acting like he wanted to tell me something, and it became apparent that he did not want Brin to hear. We placed Avar in his bed, and then Brin removed her boots and sword belt, and climbed into bed herself, taking her sheathed sword with her. Avar waited until Brin had fallen asleep and could no longer jab him in the leg with a fork, then started speaking in a drunken whisper.

"Shh. You can keep a secret, can't you, my tainted friend? I'm a Shadow Hunter," spoke the alcohol in Avar's system. The blank look on my face must have urged him to continue. "You know. A Shadow Hunter! Trained by the order to hunt down the dark creatures of the secret brood."

"Afraid I have no idea what you are saying," I responded, trying to avoid the mace, the weapon he was currently pretending to slay who knows what with.

"It's illegal, ya know. The Baron, he doesn't like faith or really any kind of power other than him. Like the other Doomed, of course, he has to deal with the others of his kind. He isn't so chummy with the ones he doesn't have in his iron clutches. The King in particular doesn't like him." He was leaning so far in towards me that I could smell the rancid brew on his breath.

Gently encouraging him to sit on his bed, I sat on the floor and asked him, "You mentioned the Doomed at dinner. Who are they?"

"What?! Everyone knows about the Doomed. They just don't talk about 'em much. Afraid they will get whisked away to be never seen again. Of course, they have reason to be afraid. The Doomed have spies everywhere. They run *everything*." The emphasis that he placed on the last word sounded volumes and told me that he and Brin were not exactly on good terms with these ominous Doomed, whoever they might be, which now meant I was likely also not on good terms with them.

Not long after Avar stopped speaking, his snoring routine began, and I found myself alone with the moonlight and my thoughts. Apart from my recollections from this past day, my mind flitted over a thousand thoughts, but didn't share anything important with my conscious self.

Lying on the firm wooden floor felt good at first, but after a few hours and Avar's snoring I restlessly sat up. I found myself staring out of the murky window at the cloudy sky. With the bright moon behind the clouds, I could see different shapes being made and unmade in their ever-changing mass. Deep in thought, I was even able to tune out Avar.

Feeling more awake that I could remember, I tried to make sense of all the things that had happened to me in the last few days. The images of the dreams felt so real that I couldn't discount them as unimportant, yet I couldn't find any way to relate them to the world I was in now. The color, smell, and the way the very air felt

Chapter 2

against my skin seemed so different in my dreams. The taste of the brew wore off and again my mouth was filled with the taste of black earth.

The moon appeared slowly from behind the clouds. It shone so brightly. In a way, it was harder to look at than the sun. With squinted eyes, I tried to look into the heart of the silvery ball, only to see more blueish white light. I couldn't help but wonder if the intensity of the sun's light didn't mask things like it did the stars. The moonlight seemed so much clearer, so much cleaner. I tip-toed between the beds towards the large window. It was deceptively tricky to open, but after a moment of trying, the window relented to my determination. The night air flowed in and seemed to caress my senses. My eyes to the heavens, I saw the stars floating in the deep black above. It felt right. I felt right. Brin sleeping quietly with her sword under her blanket, and Avar blissfully drooling slightly in his sleep; something about these two seemed like I fit. The part that disturbed me was not knowing why.

When we were at dinner, they had told me stories about their exploits, most of which I only half heard. The din of the tavern was too distracting. I envied their connection, their history. Deep in thought and entranced by the moon, I told myself I would discover the hidden parts of me.

Brin tossed relentlessly in her sleep. Occasionally the moonlight touched her skin and she seemed to turn away, whereas Avar seemed to roll towards the light, even partially hanging off his bed in order to bathe his face in its beams.

The hypnotizing power of the moon was broken as a cloud passed in front of it. The joints in my hands and knees popped and cracked as I moved, causing me to flex them more. There was certainly a strength growing within me.

Wracked

A noise came from the street and the cloud let enough moonlight in to reveal the scene below: figures moving through the shadowy empty streets all wearing the armor of the city guard, and even being led by my old chum, Larry. Frozen for a moment, I considered fleeing and leaving my two new friends behind. I moved towards the door and heard the loud knock on the front door of the inn, along with the declaration that the guard was waiting outside. Something made me look over my shoulder. I breathed in the two people in the room with me, a cold yet beautiful woman and a clumsy and boyish man. In that brief moment, I knew that for good or ill, my fate was somehow tied to theirs. There was no running from them or it. Quietly, I stepped over to Brin's bed and tried to stir her awake. As soon as whispering proved useless, I touched her shoulder.

"Sounds like last night is coming back to haunt us already." She sat up in her bed, tossing the dark curling tendrils of her hair around haphazardly. I suppose the look on my face said it all, as I had no chance to respond to her question before she leapt from the bed and strapped on her sword. "Avar! Get up!" She looked at me and I knew my uncertainty was obvious. Even though I was helpless and weak, she smiled at me anyway.

Avar muttered and stirred, but did not get up, that is, until the door splintered open. Brin stepped in front of me, pushing me towards the window. After being sprayed by chunks of door, Avar clumsily fell out of his bed and accidentally kicked his mace underneath his bed. Brin cursed under her breath and lightly kicked Avar in an attempt to motivate him.

In the doorway, one of the figures stepped forward. His sadistic smile and swollen face confirmed what I had seen from the window. "Wot do we hav heer? Looks like dem was right. You filth am gunna pay for wot you dun to Jackson and me face!"

Chapter 2

Brin didn't respond. I could see the muscles in her back tense as she readied herself for the inevitable fight. Looking down, I could only see Avar's backside and boots as he fumbled around under his bed looking for his weapon. It almost made me laugh, but that desire was quashed by Larry's command for his men, "Get 'em."

The room filled with a storm of action. Guards seemed to pour out of the doorway like ale from an upturned mug. With raging precision, Brin's blade came to life. She parried and arched through the available space trying to keep the men at bay and away from all of us. "I could use a little help, Avar!"

Mumbled words came from under the bed and then the bed flew upwards, pushing some of the guards back. Avar took only a brief moment to survey the situation before looking back to the floor and reaching down to pick up the weapon that still eluded his grasp. Brin was jumping back and forth from her bed to the floor fighting at least three or four guards. I remained in the back, near the window, helpless, and I always seemed to be in the way.

More soldiers surged into the room. Brin kicked one that charged at her and this pushed many of them backwards. In that brief moment, she tried to kick her bed frame up to create a barricade. One kick was not enough and the enemy clashed with her again, forcing her to give some ground. To give her room, I pressed myself against the window. Amidst the clatter of the combat, I heard her muttering about Avar and I turned to look over at him.

The sheer number of enemy was starting to get to Avar. His bed barricade was doing well to control the flow, but some of the soldiers were now trying to push the bed back and corner him. Their plan was working, and Avar seemed late to realize what they were doing.

Wracked

A stream of blood came near my feet. The moonlight coming through the window created a sheen that distracted me for a moment. The series of events that followed seemed to stream together into a blur. There was a sudden jarring motion and a crash, followed by a falling sensation. I looked up to see a shower of broken glass and Brin looking out the window with a horrified look on her face, then a club collided with her head. Amidst the humming glass I found serenity in the fall, but it was not to last. A loud cracking sound came from right behind my eyes and everything became black.

"Where does the darkness come from?" A wise, old voice chuckled. "The darkness comes from the absence of light. So, one might really ask, where does the light come from?"

A lit candle stood between me and the source of the voice. The intensity of light made it impossible for me to make out more than an outline of the person speaking to me. I tried to look through the bright light, and all I could see was a beard before I had to turn my eyes away from the brain searing light. Even just turning away from it, the light still was burning its way into my soul.

"You cannot run from the light, my boy. It will find you. Like most things, you have to vanquish it to be free of it."

Suddenly, I found myself running through twisting, wet stone hallways. The sounds of my own breathing and footfalls filled my ears, but were not enough to drown out the calm old voice which seemed to follow me, just as the light did. Behind me, the light seemed to obliterate everything it touched. Feeling helpless, there was nothing I could do but run from it. Somehow I knew that if light touched me, it would destroy me.

Chapter 2

"Vanquish it."

The wet stone was slippery and eventually it got the best of me. My knees crashed against the stone floor as I fell. Staring into the void of bright light, I tried to pull the tattered hood of my cloak over me as protection. In the eternal seconds that followed, I saw the beads of light piercing the spaces between the threads in my hood growing stronger and stronger until light would wash everything away, including me.

Opening my eyes, I found myself again standing on the field of red. The armored commander stood gleefully atop a mountain of corpses. Lifeless faces of children and their stewards all seemed to look at me from this horrible mountain of death. Nearby there was a flame which burned so high it seemed to be trying to escape the grip of the world. I wished I, too, could escape to a different world or even just to the sky above. The armored man laughed at me from atop his perch and sent his men towards me. At his feet I noticed a familiar beard and outline. The pangs of sorrow woke within me. These were quickly burned away by rage. The burning force of anger growing in my chest demanded to be released and I moved forward to loose my frustration and pain.

Black and purple tentacles of energy charged from my open mouth. First, they pushed forth at the sky, then writhed in the air, with my tiny body acting as their anchor to the ground. All the men stopped in their tracks, but the armored man did not even blink. After a brief pause, the tentacles leapt forward, and in a flurry of dark writhing chaos, everything was enveloped.

Wracked

My head was rocking back and forth on a cold rocky surface. Limply, my limbs were reacting to something shaking me. "Wakes up! Wakes up!" the urgent voice invaded my thoughts.

The hazy world came into focus in a flurry of blinks. The strange little man in the black cap from the night before was shaking me awake. My mind was still full of the piercing light and didn't know where I was.

"Wakes up! Wakes up befur dem mens kill you friends!"

With that quick reminder my mind reeled back to the moment of my crash through the window. I sat up to see shards of glass glinting all around me and a hole in the side of the building in front of me where a window should be. My hand brought back a trace of thick blood from the back of my head. Confused, I turned to the man in the cap. "What happened?"

"You fells frum dat window. Den dem mens took you friends to hidden place near heer! Dem sekrit spies fur da Rottin' One. Dem gunna kills you friends. I'z know wheer dem am. Quick, fallow me!"

"Wait, what? I thought this city was run by the Baron. Who is this Rotting One?"

"Dem am enemies, been fightin' fur ages. Da Rottin' One work for da King. Dem all Doomed," he said over his shoulder, and he scampered off the street and into a nearby alley. The empty street and dark windows above all led to a road alone. My mind replayed the brief moments when Brin showed me unexpected kindness. The mystery of the Doomed and these strange people urged me to follow the strange little man. Looking over my shoulde,r I caught a glimpse of blood on the street, enough to fill a bucket and all from where I had fallen.

"What happened back there to me? How did you bring me back to life?"

Chapter 2

The little man chuckled, "I'z not do nuffin, you already dead."

"I thought I was only half dead."

"Master Wrack not like dem udder 'alf deads."

Confused as I was already, this added a new layer of mystery as to who I was and how this strange little person seemed to know more about me than I did. Before I could harass my guide with more questions, we stopped.

"Dem in dat cellar."

Looking where he was pointing, I saw a dark building with a tiny glow coming from the cellar windows. From where we were, the stairs to the cellar were obvious and completely unguarded. Focusing my attention on the cellar, I could hear shouting and the random sounds of something hard hitting something wet.

Each time the beating sound assaulted my ears, I ground my teeth together. "How am I going to get them out of there? I don't have a weapon or anything," I said, but I was talking to myself. The little man in the cap had vanished.

I crept up to one of the windows. Inside, I saw a few dark figures moving around some barrels and crates in the room. In the center of the room was a chair with a slumped form tied to it. The mocking laughter of that fat, bald guard drifted out of the cellar like a rank odor. My hands grew cold, and my face carved itself into a scowl. I wasn't sure how I was going to save Brin and Avar, but I knew I couldn't just sit outside and listen to them get beat to death.

As I moved from my hiding place to the stairs, my hands got colder and I felt a horrible stinging in them. My robes fluttered as I quickly stepped down to the dark doorway. My uncertainty held me back for a moment, but my resolve was steeled as I heard more of the beating sounds and the mocking laughter. I pushed open the door.

Wracked

Three steps into the room and I barely even had their attention. Avar lay tied up in the corner of the room, looking worse for wear. There was a pool of dark blood under the chair that Brin was tied to. The three men in the room muttered something about me closing the door and continued looming over Brin.

"Who you workin' for? Is da Prince makin' a play for Yellow Liva?" Larry shouted at Brin.

One of the other men raised a mailed fist to continue the beating.

Sternly I said, "Stop that."

He looked over at me with a confused and angry look, which quickly changed to confused and a little afraid.

"Wha—You're dead! Your head wuz all bustid open!" Larry's mocking laughter was nowhere to be found.

All of these men who were guards, spies, and seasoned warriors for some ominous doomed overlord stood dumbfounded at my sudden appearance. We stood looking at each other until Larry noticed that I had no weapon, then the horrible laugh began again. "I ain't sure 'ow you live thru dat fall or da stabbin' we gaves ya. Dis time, we not gunna mess it up."

All the guards drew their weapons and cautiously started to move toward me. Brin spit out a mouthful of blood and whispered, "Run." Larry's rage was unleashed upon her with a loud cracking slap across her face. A spray of blood flew across the room and smacked against the stone floor.

The anger I had growing in my gut twisted and churned. It felt like a nest of dark worms all trying to force their way out of a small bag. The yell that came out of my mouth felt like I was back in that dream. The monster within me rose behind my eyes and I drank in the fear I saw in the faces of the guards, especially Larry. A cold rush seemed to wash around me and the room was filled

Chapter 2

with lashing black and purple tendrils of energy. Horrified screams of the guardsmen sang to my soul as I listened to them suffering within the writhing tendrils. The air around me became suffocating and the tendrils began to crush me. Within a moment, there was another cold rush and the energy was gone. The exhaustion of fighting against the tendrils made me collapse to the floor. From across the room I met Avar's frightened eyes.

Wracked

Chapter 3

The room felt empty. Bodies of the guards stared into space with terror frozen in their lifeless eyes. Avar's squirming washed away the silence left in the void after the darkness abated. My mind asked the question, *Had that power come from me?* All I had to do was follow Avar's frightened look to answer the question.

Standing in the open doorway behind me were three figures, all wearing black robes. One of them pulled his hood back to reveal the funny old man with the black cap. There was something ominous and powerful about the three men, a feeling I had not felt in the presence of the old man the two times we met before. I think they sensed my apprehension or curiosity, because they waited for me to speak first; however, it wasn't me who ended up breaking the silence. Brin mustered enough strength to shake her chair and say, "Uzkin' untie me already!!"

The four of us in robes moved to untie both Avar and Brin. I looked at her battered face, which held strength even in its broken state. Her raw determination and ferocity resonated somewhere inside me, as if I used to be like her in one way or another and had forgotten how to be so strong. When she saw my face, there was a little smile hidden in her impatience and her eager desire to be unbound. As soon as she was free, she tried to stand. When she wavered slightly, she grabbed my robe and steadied herself. I wanted to whisper to her something witty, like now we are even, but I didn't. She steadied herself and spit out some more blood, then started looking for her gear. Avar, who seemed less damaged, found their stuff, and they started to redress.

One of the taller robe figures came over to me and said, "Master, soon they will come looking for you and your companions. You should flee the city."

"Can't leave yet. I have a lead here about my father." Brin's aggressive charms leapt into the conversation.

"I am afraid that you haven't much time to follow up on any 'leads'. These men were spies and the city itself is in danger. Soon the whole place will be locked down. You must flee," he said to Brin, before turning and looking at me. His grey eyes looking deep into mine as if we were not strangers. Around his neck was a necklace with a black sun with eight silver rays and a spiral etched into the heart of the sun. "Master, you must find the Shadow within the forest. It is only there you might know the next steps to take."

Confused, I just nodded my head and the three men smoothly retreated through the door. Avar was able to capture my feelings with a very astute observation. "Well, that was strange."

Unwilling to accept the advice of our strange saviors, Brin searched the pockets of our fat ex-nemesis. Within his pockets she found something that convinced her that our new friends might be right. "Let's head to the forest. Maybe this Shadow is the person I have been looking for anyway."

It was not yet dawn, but the streets of Yellow Liver were starting to wake up. Hard working people pushed carts through the streets while those who had nothing were already stirring to beg for help or at least one more ale to ease their pain. At first our flight through the streets was rapid, as if there were some horrible, shapeless beast chasing us. We realized that no one was immediately

Chapter 3

upon us and our pace slowed. As the first light that heralded the coming of the dawn appeared, Brin and Avar started to argue about which way would be the best out of the city.

"Brin, why are we going this way?" Avar asked. "The west gate will put us right on the road to the exit."

"I know what I am doing, Avar. How many times have I saved our skins by running in circles?"

Resentment filled Avar's deep sigh. "Right. Confuse, distract, disappear. Maybe this time warrants a more direct fleeing action. It won't be long before the city is on to us."

"You give these uzkin' idiots too much credit."

Being of no use to such a discussion, I became distracted by watching the city coming to life before me, people leaving their homes to start their daily struggle to survive, some with families to wish them fortune in the day's toil, and others with nothing but an empty home that they left behind. Even those with family were gripped by an unspoken fear; the difficulty of life here within the gates of the city was not much better than the life that those children had outside the walls. My mind wandered through questions about the attacks of those ghoul things outside the gate, and I wondered if that happened inside the gates. It occurred to me that the guards did nothing during the attacks outside, and I could not help but wonder if there was a connection between the ghouls and whatever Doomed power ran this place. Some questions are answered faster than you are ready for.

The purple sky was smeared with charcoal clouds above us. Our quiet flight to escape the city took an unexpected turn when Avar heard a guard whistle and urged us to start running. It didn't take long for the guards to find us. Sooner than we would have liked, there were armored men wearing the black tabard of the

Wracked

Baron chasing us through the streets. No one we passed would even look at us. Most just went inside the nearest building and pretended that nothing was going on in the street near them.

"We're going the wrong way!" Avar insisted.

"When have I ever let you down, Avar? Trust my instincts! Follow me."

Helpless as I felt, I had no choice but to trust her. Putting his concern and fear in check, Avar continued to follow her. Through alleyways and narrow streets, we fled. At times it felt like a sea of soldiers chased us. A pounding in my head made it even harder to remain calm. My thoughts went inward again, and I realized that the pounding was my heart racing. *The old man said I was dead, though. How could my heart be beating?* And with this small distraction, Avar and Brin somehow escaped my view.

Immediately, I felt the panic setting in. My feet stopped running and I scanned the crowd for Brin's dark trail of hair or Avar tripping over some passerby. Each way I looked, I was met with scowls and disapproving looks from the denizens of the city. An urgent clatter of boots whispered in my direction. Like rats fleeing a sinking ship, the curiosity of the people standing in the tiny marketplace was overwhelmed by a desire to save their own skins. A handful of black tabard clad guardsmen came running into the marketplace. When they set eyes on me, their running slowed.

"Well, well. I is gunna get a reward for dis one, I am." His greasy hair and dark teeth gave away the truth of the man I now faced, wearing the new looking guard uniform. "Oi! I found da one you lookin' for!"

The confusion as to who the greasy weasel was calling out to was abated by first the smell of rotting flesh, then the appearance of a grey skinned human-like creature with strong arms and a permanent reddish-black stain around its mouth. Tattered and

Chapter 3

stained remnants of clothing hung on its lithe form. Instantly, I knew I was finally getting a good look at one of the horrors that was stealing children from outside the city walls. My back straightened; the creature's malice was a stink that was nearly as strong as the smell of death that surrounded it. A twisted smile revealed sharp, brown pointed teeth and further broadcast that he wasn't after Brin or Avar, but me.

I readied myself for the creature's attack as the guardsmen all smirked and parted for the thing to awkwardly slink through the small crowd of them that now surrounded me. I looked around trying to find where I might be able to make an escape. The only ready way out was if I could turn into a bird and fly, but even in my imagination I couldn't see that actually happening. A hissing, gurgling sound brought me back to my predicament and was followed by the grey skinned thing leaping at me. As before, when facing my attackers in the alley, I found myself reacting to the attack by stepping out of the way. The creature growled in discontentment, but the sickening grin explained that it relished a challenge. Uncertain what to do next, I moved around the circle like I was some sort of arena wrestler. We circled each other for a few moments, with the guards cheering the creature on.

"Ghoul" was the word I kept catching them call this grey thing I was facing Ghoul. My memory went back to my conversations over the last day. I could swear someone said something about ghouls, how ghouls ran the city for the Baron, or something. My internal distraction gave my opponent an opening. He came flying at me with great speed, all teeth and flailing claws. My side was torn open as I tried to twirl away. Pain now pulled me out of my head. Anger flooded my veins and I found myself truly in the fight. More flurries of claws and gnashing teeth came at me. My hand found a hold at one of the creature's wrists and I flipped him over. The innate nimbleness of the ghoul was astounding as it just continued to roll back into its normal hunched stance. A few more times we locked and I escaped before the thought occurred to me, *Can I even win this fight?*

Again my opponent took advantage of my insecurity, and this time dug something small and black into my open wounds. Burning and deep went the ghouls weapon into me, and I felt its weapon draining something from me. Thoughts that lay dormant, but present, were stolen from me. Only the void they left behind told me that they were gone. After what seemed like an eternity the weapon was removed from my side, and I collapsed to the ground. The ghoul stood looming over me, his clawed hand covered in my dark blood, a black talon in his clutches. The talon seemed to be drinking in the blood on its surface. The ghoul used its black tongue to lick some of my blood off of its claws before gurgling out a small laugh.

There I lay at the mercy of the ghoul and his men, yet instead of finishing me off it made a motion with its claw and they all left. A few of the guards spat at me or mocked me as they walked away. One of my hands reached down to the wound at my side. The exposed bone and flesh were repairing themselves rapidly and my hand returned with only a smear of dark blood on my fingers. Befuddled at everything that had just happened to me, I could not help but question if I could be killed. My instinct was to ask Avar about it, but I feared his response, perhaps labeling me as one of the 'shadows' that he lived to exterminate.

"Wrack!"

"Here!" I responded as I tried to stand up, my limbs still slightly numb from the draining attack of the ghoul's black talon.

Chapter 3

Brin and Avar came rushing into the market expecting a fight and looking every which way for the guardsmen and finding none. Standing up straight, I still felt the dizzying void in my thoughts, and I tried to shake it off.

"You ok?" asked Avar with genuine concern.

"Yeah. Let's get the uzk out of here."

"Sounds like my kinda plan," Brin said as she took back the point position and led us away from the marketplace. Behind us, the curious people of the city watched us disappear into the winding narrow streets and were left with only a small dark stain on the stone of the market.

We still moved as if we were being pursued, even though I knew they were no longer chasing us. This fact I did not share with my companions, mostly because I was afraid of their response. Brin found a storm drain around the west wall of the city, and we washed out of the city with the refuse and garbage. Before long, Yellow Liver was just a black scar on the horizon as we headed west.

By dawn the next morning, Avar had had enough of the stench of the water we climbed through to make our escape. His complaints forced Brin into finding a pool of sulfur-smelling water in the rocky hills nearby. We took turns bathing and washing our clothes. The sulfur wasn't much better than the stink we carried around, but at least it was easier to get used to. This being the first time I had truly been disrobed, I took a moment to look for scars or marks on my body. There were some scars here and there. but no marks specifically from the various wounds that I remember receiving. There was a tiny black mark I thought I saw on my side, possibly the edge of a tattoo that I couldn't completely see. The fact that I couldn't see it and that I didn't know what it meant bothered me. The idea of showing Avar or Brin to the tattoo made me further uncomfortable. I made sure to not put my exposed back to either of my companions.

Brin took her turn in the smelly water and left Avar and me facing the other way. My guilt, paranoia, and curiosity compelled me to try and learn more about the world I had woken up into, so I started pestering Avar.

"Tell me more about these Doomed you mentioned before."

He gave me a startled look for a moment. I don't think he remembered talking about them before. "There is a lot to tell. Not sure specifically what I said before. So. . . There are supposedly thirteen Doomed. They are all linked by some magical thing that they did several thousand years ago."

"Magical thing?"

"Yeah. Legend calls it 'The Breaking of the World' or 'The Cursing'. Supposedly it is their fault that crops won't grow, animals die, water is poisonous, cities fell into the ground, and the air became toxic. Sounds like a bunch of paranoia if you ask me, but they certainly aren't good for the people living under their thumb."

"How did they end up in power?"

"Well, I am not sure anyone knows specifically what happened during the Cursing, but they were all mortal men once. When they did whatever it was that they did to the world, they all joined forces to destroy their enemies and crushed everyone. After there was no one left to conquer, as the story says, they turned on each other. Some of them are now slaves or minions to other Doomed."

Chapter 3

Things that he said the other night started to make more sense. I nodded to show him that I was still engaged, but I am not sure it even mattered, he was so absorbed in sharing information. Brin was probably tired of hearing it all, and so Avar seemed happy to have someone new to teach.

"What about Yellow Liver?" I asked.

"Oh, that place is owned by The Baron, who is one of the most powerful of all the Doomed. His livery is the black tabard with the red trim. Sometimes you might even see it with a red skull, minus its bottom jaw." Avar showed me sketches of symbols from his book as he talked. "Yellow Liver is supposedly directly held by The Ghoul, but I have never heard of anyone who has seen him."

"I think I might have, or one of his minions anyway."

Avar's face lit up. "Really? Like one of his ghouls? Most of the Doomed create creatures similar to them. Well, the weaker ones anyway. Where did you see him?"

"When I was outside the city, I saw a bunch of hunched creatures stealing children. I think they called them ghouls."

His eyes became slits as if he didn't believe me. While part of what I told him was a lie, I hoped that there was enough truth in it to get past his defenses.

"Hrm. They probably were. Ghouls have a taste for flesh, and I suppose the young of people who won't be missed are the easiest targets." There was a hint of sorrow in his voice. In his eyes there was some lingering regret. He looked away for a long time before speaking again. "Anyway. Shadow Hunters, like me, exist to try and fight off the corruption and darkness that the Doomed have brought to the world. Too long have people been held silently in their thrall."

"Are there a lot of Shadow Hunters?"

Wracked

"Not that many anymore. Most of us were killed off during at the battle of Black Tree. Those of us that remain are still trying to make a difference."

"Most of you that are left are fools." Brin's voice burst into the conversation and made me laugh for some reason.

"Yeah, well. Some of us might be fools, but you still offered to let me work with you." Avar said, sheepishly.

"The Shadow Hunters are some of the best lore keepers I have ever come across. I am using you for your knowledge." Her comment even made Avar laugh.

In the silence that followed, I appreciated the dynamic of my two new friends. Brin was hard and harsh, but Avar's generous nature allowed him to take her spiky exterior in stride. Some part of me hoped I could add something to our friendship. While I was off in thought, I apparently was staring over at Brin, because her sharp tongue commented, "Any more of that, and I might have to start charging you." My head quickly snapped away and I continued my conversation with Avar.

"Who do you think those black-robed fellows were?"

"I dunno. Unless I am mistaken, they called you master, so I was hoping you could clue *me* in." Avar's grin was a little smug.

Recalling one of the few distinguishing things about them I said, "There was a symbol around one of their necks. It looked like a black sun with eight silver rays and a silver spiral in the middle."

This piqued Avar's curiosity, and he made me draw the symbol on the rocky clay that we were sitting on. Once I did, he grew very quiet and retrieved the very same book he had shown me images from. He flipped through the pages for an hour or so, long enough that Brin finished her bath and rejoined us on the rocks. She smiled at me and offered to share some of her packed food. Hunger

Chapter 3

wasn't something that I had yet experienced, but I took some of her food and ate it. The taste was bland and unappealing, and when I was finished I had no desire to have anymore.

"Ah ha!" Avar exclaimed. "The black sun is a symbol that was used in the ritual that cursed the world. But other than that, I have no idea what it means and there is no spiral in the middle of it. I think that means those guys were working for one of the Doomed."

"What does your book say about my father's sword?" She asked him, already knowing the answer.

"Uh, nothing."

Sounding like a cynical mother teaching her child, "Right. Everyone works for the Doomed, Avar. Even the Shadow Hunters probably have a secret link to them."

He couldn't hide the wound that last comment gave him. With Avar not communicating, there was an awkward silence. Brin obviously did not feel like she needed to apologize, and Avar didn't know how to respond, so it was up to me to break the silence.

"So, if you don't care about the black robed men, why are you taking me to the forest?"

"If I didn't help you, no one would. You would be lost out here." Brin said, matter of factly.

"Oh."

She continued, "And, this Shadow might know something about my father."

"I couldn't help but notice, you keep bringing him up."

Brin sighed. The look on her face told me that she really didn't like the fact that I was prying into her past, and it was impossible for me to ignore.

"Sorry. Wasn't my intention to make you uncomfortable."

Wracked

There was an uncomfortable distain in her face, "Just not something I enjoy talking about."

The entire time I had known Brin, she had been bringing up her father. A blind man could see that something about her father was what drove her. It seemed odd to me that she was unwilling to open up about something that she was seeking so intently. Knowing that she would just deflect or get angry, I let the subject die. Three of us sat in silence, resting there near the sulfur pools, as the day grew closer to its fullness. Avar and Brin took turns napping to regain some of their strength. I was not tired, so I didn't sleep. I thought a lot during the time that I was alone. The chain of events that led me from my hidden sleep to here I searched and searched for some detail, something I had missed to explain more about who I was or how I had ended up here. The secrets of my past eluded me. I was trying to solve a puzzle without having all the pieces. It was infinitely frustrating.

Around the time that the sun started its decline Brin stood up and said, "Let's move." We climbed over dusty rocks, and stumbled through twisted brush that tore at our clothing. Brin seemed accustomed to traveling off the roads and it was obvious that Avar had been traveling with her for a while. It didn't take me long to find my traveling stride. It helped that I rarely felt the exhaustion that even Brin had, though she tried to hide it. During the course of the next several days, we shared some moments of open and friendly competition between us. It was only in this competition that I saw Brin smile, outside of the few times it seemed like she was secretly smiling at me. The difference in the moments we shared led me to believe that perhaps I saw smiles when there were none.

Several days went by over rough terrain. When we crested a yellowish rocky hill with spots of brown grass, we saw the immense ominous forest that was our destination. My eyes took in

Chapter 3

the misty and forbidding horizon. Mountains became the far wall of our world with what looked like a tremendous amount of snow covered trees. The snow and mist only seemed to hover over the trees, however. There was no white on the dark ground of the forest.

"Webs." Avar's voice had a sense of dread in it. "The forest is supposedly full of spiders. Never been there myself, but I hear they are huge."

"Never met a spider I couldn't kill."

This sort of morbid response I had grown to expect from Brin. Part of me wondered if she just had a dark sense of humor, or if she were really that cold. "How do you think we will find this Shadow person when we get there?"

"No idea," Avar responded. "I assume that we will stumble on it somehow. Things have a way of finding you when you look for them loud enough."

Brin chuckled, "Yeah, and stealth has never been your strongest skill."

The genuine, kind, and humorous nature of Avar continued to astound me. This insult was tiny and meaningless, but her assault upon his character was relentless. This moment, for whatever reason, made me glad that I found myself in the company of two diverse and interesting people. I tried to imagine what it would be like to have ended up being Larry's friend. Lots of brutal beatings and backstabbing was all I could think of. Drifting to another place I wondered about the boy outside the walls of Yellow Liver, and about the ghoul that attacked me in the streets of the city. I remembered how I entered the city to help the boy, and there was a question in my mind if I was on the right path to that end. Furthermore, I wondered if my keeping that attack a secret from Avar and Brin was the best idea.

Wracked

Camp was made and a fire started. I sat and watched Avar and Brin eat the small birds that Brin had caught a few hours earlier. I felt separate from them in that moment. Watching them satisfy a hunger that I knew in name only, the fact that I was not really human bubbled to the surface of my thoughts. With everything else rolling around in my skull, I wanted to connect. Before I could stop myself I blurted out, "I was attacked by a ghoul."

Immediately after I said it, I started playing with a stick in the fire. Secretly hoping that neither of them had heard me. When I looked back up, they had both stopped eating and were staring at me.

"When?" Brin asked.

"Remember when you lost me in the streets when we were running?"

Disbelief filled Brin's face, "You were only gone for a minute, how could you have gotten attacked?"

"I dunno. It seemed like they were coming for me. There were all these guards and a grey skinned thing with them. Before I knew what was going on, it was all over me."

Brin laughed. "You are kidding right? This is some kind joke."

"I don't think he is kidding," fear danced in Avar's voice.

"I'm not. I got attacked. It clawed me up pretty good. Stabbed me right here with a big black talon thing. I guess when it heard you guys coming, they all ran."

Brin's face became similar to the look on Larry's when he was demanding answers from her. "Why didn't you tell us about this earlier? I mean, you don't even have any wounds," she said, motioning to her bruised face. "This is all very weird."

Chapter 3

"Calm down, Brin," Avar said as he tried to do the same. "There is obviously more going on here than we are aware of. Wrack, did you have wounds? Was the thing able to hurt you?"

"Yeah, I even left a bit of blood on the street. When I checked later though, the wound was gone."

There was sudden realization in Avar's eyes, "That explains how you were able to survive the fall from the inn. You certainly are an interesting creature, Wrack."

"Uzk! Interesting? Interesting!? You don't even know who or what you are, do you? Uzk! We are going into the Forest of Shadows with someone who might be the living uzkin' dead and you are just uzkin' interested? Aren't you a Shadow Hunter, Avar? Why do I get the feeling that you are going to be the death of us, Wrack? Huh?"

I wasn't expecting this outpouring of fear and anger. Stunned into silence, I wasn't sure what to say next. Luckily, Avar picked that up and decided to speak instead.

"Quit overreacting, Brin. You said yourself you felt you saved Wrack for a reason. I try to trust in your instincts and so do you usually. From my conversations with Wrack, his situation is as puzzling to him as it is to us. I—"

"That's uzking comforting," she blurted out.

My emotions got the better of me and I interjected without thinking, "I am not trying to make you uncomfortable. For what it is worth, I appreciate everything you have done for me. I only wish there were something I could do to show you both."

Brin wasn't sure exactly what to say. Her sharp tongue seemed without anything or anyone to cut, and her frustration drove her into an angry silence that was so overpowering, none of us talked for the rest of the night.

Wracked

In the dark reaches of the night, I found myself staring at the blackness where I knew the forest to be. I felt that same longing to change things. The idea of leaving the two sleeping people I sat watch over, Brin's failed desire to keep watch over me all night notwithstanding, was just something I couldn't do. It was my fault they were here, and I couldn't bring myself to abandon them. In addition, it seemed that Avar might be my only chance of solving the puzzle that was my own existence. I couldn't run away from that.

The morning came with the usual pain from the overwhelming light of the sun and we silently packed our camp. Brin was still fuming about the conversation the night before. Avar was even more awkward because he wasn't sure how to resolve it. When we were all ready, Brin set out ahead of us to lead the way. This time she went a little further than usual. Occasionally, I could hear her talking to herself in angry whispers.

"Don't worry about it. Brin is a little screwed up," Avar explained. "Happens when you watch your father get murdered when you are a small child. Changed her whole life in that moment, I expect. When she talks about it, it almost seems like there are two people in her head: one who is cold and ruthlessly bent on revenge, the other who is tired and wants it all to be over. Not sure if she even thinks there can be a happy ending for her. So, you can see how she has problems trusting people."

Hearing intimate details about someone from another person is awkward. I wasn't sure how I should respond to all this information, so I just remained quiet.

"Anyway," he continued. "I am sure she needs some time alone, but I think she will get over it. She really likes you. She must, because she doesn't ever stick her neck out for anyone. At least

Chapter 3

not unless it suits her. I was shocked when she told me how she helped you. Very unlike her. And there is always the fact that I am completely intrigued by your situation, Wrack. Hopefully we—"

"Who killed her father?"

Avar took a second to adjust to my interruption. "She doesn't know. Late one night, she got really drunk and started babbling about some conspiracy that involved the Doomed and her father, but I don't know how much of it is true."

Avar kept talking, but I wasn't listening anymore. My eyes kept looking at the dark haired woman who we were following. If what Avar said were true, then I could not help but feel that Brin and I had more in common than was obvious. Both searching for something unimaginable in a life that we don't quite understand and where we feel alone. Just saving her life wasn't enough for me anymore. I wanted her life to mean something. In that moment I resolved to help her find what she was looking for with whatever power I could muster.

We drew closer and closer to the looming forest. From a distance it looked like a tangle of brown and black smears dusted with a coating of translucent white lace. The distance tricked my eyes about the immensity of the forest. As we came up upon it I saw how truly colossal the trees of the wood were, dark, almost black, covered in twisting vines and dead branches. Where you would expect to find leaves were layers and layers of webbing. Wispy fine lines and tough strong ropes of webbing wound their way around the giant net that was the canopy of the forest. Dark spots within the webbing contained secrets that made my mind buzz with curiosity. Perhaps it contained a nest of spiders as large as dogs, or the remains of some small army that found their resting place in a silky white tomb in the sky.

My contemplation was broken by Avar shaking me.

Wracked

"Hey, have you always not had a shadow?" He was pointing at the ground near my feet.

Following his finger, I looked down and saw that Avar was right. While he had a shadow from the sun nearing the horizon, I decidedly did not. Brin heard what Avar said and came over to see what we were staring at. While there were three of us standing on the grassy field leading the forest, there were only two shadows stretched across the ground, trying to escape the painful rays of the sun.

"Creepy," was all I could think to say.

Chapter 4

Cutting through the barrier of brush, webs, and dead limbs was time consuming but easily done. Inside the forest was like another world. Columns of light boldly breached the canopy above our heads. The translucent webs defused the light and gave everything a constant feeling of twilight. Shadows loomed in the corners everywhere, even in our minds. Every few moments Avar would jump at the sight of something that wasn't there, or would insist he heard noises that we couldn't. Eventually Brin told him firmly and quietly to "Shut the uzk up." If Brin didn't know where we were going, she sure faked it well.

While the outside made it look like the forest was dense, the trees were actually so huge that they had space enough for entire battalions to march between them. The spaces between were sparsely filled with fallen wisps of webbing or dark brush. Travel through the musty decaying underworld of the forest was spooky to say the least, and the random cold, light breeze didn't help.

Deeper and deeper we went into the eerie quiet. Shuffling noises came from above us. Avar's tongue couldn't stay at bay. "What was that? Was that us?"

Brin was scanning the canopy. My eyes tried to track where she was looking. "It was nothing, Avar," she lied and pressed on.

Wracked

As we drew into the shadowy heart of the forest it grew colder. Mist caressed our feet as we trampled through the webs and decaying underbrush. Days went by in the sleepy quiet of the darkness. If Brin did not know the way she certainly hid that from us. Ever present was Avar's paranoia, slowly grinding away at even Brin's steely resolve. Skittering and whispered shuffling from the canopy above gradually became as common as the cold breeze which gave life to the webs all around us.

"I mean, really," Avar's whispered voice wavered with fear. "There have to be spiders here. Look at all the webs. Wha—what was that?!"

"Shut the uzk up!" Brin hissed.

Avar's fear of our unseen hosts would be quieted for a few hours and then his thoughts would seize control of his tongue once again, only to receive more abuse from Brin's. Moments before Avar would start complaining, he would begin whispering to himself. When Brin figured that out, she was even more efficient in silencing him before he began shouting. After a while it was amusing. I, too, looked for evidence of any spidery masters of this place, other than the obvious webs, but all I ever saw were unmoving dark spots within the weave above. I told myself they were just the trees blocking the light.

More days went by and I thought to question our leader, but I did not wish to cause any more static between us. Maybe it was a little callous of me, but I couldn't help but think, *it wouldn't be me that went hungry if we ran out of food in this desolate place.* Both of them had begun to resort to the dried grain and fruits they carried with them for sustenance. The thought eventually struck me that I would rather see them starve due to Brin's negligence than try and correct her. The lack of good prey was making her even more

Chapter 4

difficult to deal with than usual. She started sleeping in more, and her temper was even shorter than normal. One night I even think I heard her weeping softly in her sleep.

Occasionally in the strange glow of the night, I would practice talking to Brin, trying to find how to talk to her about her father and promise to help her. "Seems like there is a lot the same in our lives," I would whisper to myself. "Neither one of us really knows where things will lead us, and we are both driven to some purpose which is probably different than either of us expect."

After one of these nights Brin was calmer than usual and actually let Avar lead for a little while. She walked beside me for a time, and each time I looked over at her she would either smile or look away quickly. A fool is the only person that couldn't have picked up on what was going on, and I was a fool. Still, somehow my whispering in the dark had gotten to her ears and she accepted it, but waited for me to actually say something to her. I did not.

One particularly jumpy and hungry day, Avar was leading us. We seemed to be walking for hours and I kept thinking I was seeing the same tree over and over again. Turning to Brin I was going to ask her if we were still going the right way, but when I opened my mouth to speak, the expectant look on her face slaughtered my words before they could even be formed. When I looked away, I think I even heard her giggle.

"Where the uzk are you taking us, Avar? The ruins are this way, and you are leading us in a circle."

"Fine! You lead." He threw his hands in the air, "I keep thinking I am seeing fresh tracks anyway. Probably just us."

"Fresh tracks? What the uzk are you talkin' about. There is nothing here, Avar. I keep telling you that there is noth—"

Wracked

Before the rest of the word could even travel the complex labyrinth of her mind to get to her mouth there was an impact. The blur of movement collided into Brin throwing her off to one side and she skillfully rolled upright, drawing her sword as she turned to face the large black mangy wolf that now crouched in the middle of our small company. When she thought our attentions were turned to the wolf, I saw her put her free hand on a hidden wound on her sword arm and wince.

The wolf itself had massive forward legs and shoulders, making its hind quarters less impressive in comparison. The growls and snarls that came from it also had a strange hiss hidden in with the other sounds. Ignoring Brin, the wolf padded around towards Avar and me with his eyes transfixed on me. My face relaxed and I felt all tension fade from me and I looked directly into my predator's eyes. They were slitted, like that of a bird's, and as it got closer there was a horrible stink that I could only imagine came from the large patches of exposed diseased skin on its hide.

The ground rustled as Brin twisted around to see two more wolves flanking her. She retreated from them slowly, trying to consolidate our position. Avar moved with the wolf that was fixed on me. He kept himself between us with weapon drawn, anticipating an attack. Moments later, the three of us were being circled by the three sickly looking beasts. I could feel Brin growing restless from the stalemate. Looking away from the wolves, for a moment I glanced over at Avar. The look on his face was the same as some of the parents of the poor children outside the city, manifesting itself when the child had done something exceptionally naughty. One of the wolves sensed that I was distracted and took a swipe at me. I leapt back and narrowly escaped the massive black claws of the beast. It snarled in disappointment.

Chapter 4

"How long are they going to do this, Avar?" Patience was not one of her strengths.

"No idea. I don't know why they haven't just killed us all already."

"Killed us? Way to be optimistic there, Avar."

"You know what I mean."

My eyes never drifted away from the nearest wolf. After that last attack, I did not want to give them another opportunity to get me.

"You with me, Avar?" More of a statement than a question, and I knew what was coming next.

"You're the boss," he said in practiced reply.

Not sure if she actually waited for the whole sentence to get into the air before she lashed out with her sword at the wolf in front of her. Taken unaware by the attack, the wolf backed off a little bit and gave a little yelp. Avar, too, swung his mace at the nearest wolf, cracking it across the jaw. It was a wonderful hit, considering that he swung at it with his eyes closed.

Dirt, sticks, and dusty webs were kicked up in the violence that ensued. My attention had to return to the wolf that was on me. When it lunged, I twirled around and escaped its attack, but also found myself outside the previous circle of action. Brin shot me a look of disappointment and drew closer to stand back to back with Avar. From their stories, I knew that this was a style that they were accustomed to using.

The wolf lunged again at me, and I leaned out of the attack and punched it in the side as I ran around it. The hit seemed to startle it more than it did any damage, and I ran behind a nearby tree. Stalking me in the trees seemed to be this wolf's dream come true, as it gave me a glimpse of itself and then sneaked quickly around the other side of the tree. When I tried to stop and turn, I

Wracked

slid on the decayed underbrush and almost fell as I turned and tried to run. Deftly, the wolf's teeth found their mark on my ankle. Pain rippled from the deep wounds in my flesh and when they reached my mouth the ripples became a scream.

Using the leverage it had over me, it whipped me backwards. Bones in my leg popped and more pain caused more noise. From my new position, I saw Brin delivering a killing stroke to her wolf across its neck as it tried to jump at her. I blinked and then saw Avar standing over the corpse of his wolf with a sad look on his face. Again my attacker shook me with its powerful jaws and started dragging me behind a tree. My leg inside the creature's mouth could feel its tongue recoiling from my flesh and a moment later, it let me go.

Flipping around to keep my eyes on the wolf, I saw it shaking its head and coughing like it had just tasted that rancid brew from the Headless Mermaid. Using my arms to drag myself away from the wolf, I heard Brin call for me and I responded. The wolf stopped coughing and again began growling at me. Its posture changed to make me think that he was about to pounce on me again. Rustling came from behind me. I saw the power of the creature's legs when all the fur on its body shook as it leapt off the ground at me. I rolled out of the way and against the tree. As I scrambled to sit up against the tree, the wolf's mouth was inches away from my face. Years of unwashed gore and sickness invaded my nostrils as it moved in for the kill. A whooshing sound made the side of the wolf explode, and I was covered in warm dark blood then the corpse of the wolf fell on me.

The three of us pushed the body off me and Brin's insight forced her to speak, "We gotta get you a weapon. I am tired of saving your ass all the time."

Chapter 4

Our injuries were counted immediately after as we made camp. Brin's shoulder was bruised from her landing, Avar had a nasty gash on his thigh from his fight, and me with a chewed ankle. Avar tended to his wounds while Brin helped me with mine. She called it cleaning the wound, but I could swear she was enjoying the pain it was bringing me too much. She kept telling me not to be a baby when I would gasp or clench my teeth. She even poked the wound once on purpose.

"That doesn't hurt."

"Yeah, it does."

"I am just trying to help. If you don't want me to clean the wound, I can go rest my shoulder."

I grabbed her hand before she could get away from me. "No. Help me, please."

Smiling as she returned to tending my wound, she broke up some plants and placed them in the wound, then wrapped some cloth over it from her own sleeve. "That should make it heal quickly. Hopefully you will be okay to walk by the morning."

"Thanks." I could feel the wounds healing in the darkness of the bandage already. Something kept me from saying anything to her.

"Welcome." There was that smile again, with a small glimmer in her eye. I didn't want her to walk away from me, but I did nothing to stop her. She turned and the smell of her hair drifted in my direction filling me with a tiny bit of bliss, or was that the herb she had me chew before going to work on me?

That night, my senses came to life. There was no way I could have known that my sense of smell had been muted. The night air refreshed me and the cold renewed my lungs. After a couple of

Wracked

deep breaths, taking in the misty cold air, I coughed a little, and some black wet dirt came up. With this blockage removed, my breath was freed. I closed my eyes and I could smell everything.

Wet bark on the trees, the decay of the underbrush, the soil underneath, the insects crawling in that soil; I could smell everything. From sitting on the other side of our campsite, I could smell the earthy oils that Brin rubbed into her skin every day. From Avar, I smelled the sweet incense that he carried and the old pages of that book. Even more curious about what the book contained, I thought of sneaking over to him and taking it from his belt where it was chained. A devious part of me was convinced that the secrets to who I was lay within its hidden pages. Before the scheme could finish itself, I could smell the day coming and I was so distracted by the way the air changed from moment to moment that I surrendered my desire to read Avar's precious book.

The light was at first just like tiny candles hanging in the canopy, slowly growing more intense, then turned into the lances piercing the thick webbing above. The scents of the forest changed as the air was warmed slightly. An unusual smell seemed to loom over us. It was like a wonderful and subtle perfume which had grown old and stagnant. Looking up into the webs, I wondered what that smell could be coming from.

My wounds had healed completely, and I removed the medicine that Brin had placed under the bandages, leaving my wrappings in place. Shortly after, we were all up and about.

"Feel well enough to travel?" Brin asked.

Without seeing to whom the question was addressed, Avar answered, "Yeah, I think I am ok."

"That's great Avar, but I was asking Wrack."

"Oh."

Chapter 4

My mouth curled into a smile and I said, "I am fine. Let's get moving."

Our leader kept taking us into the colder part of the woods, then she saw something in the dirt and hummed something lightly to herself, looking around. Quickly, she decided to go in a slightly different direction. As we travelled, I felt the cold coming from behind me and something told me that we were going the wrong way. I assumed that Brin knew the way and held back my concern.

Trees and brush grew tighter around us and soon we were back to chopping and pushing our way through grasping thorns and sliding between closely growing trees. Then I saw it. Light. Light coming from beyond the trees. It seemed touched with a stronger intensity of white than was on the other side of the forest. I had given up on counting the days we were traveling in the woods, so I do not have any idea how far away we were from where we entered, but that wasn't what was bothering me.

"I see sunlight up ahead."

Brin responded with a softness that I never heard her have with Avar, "Yeah, I see it, too."

"Didn't those men say that the Shadow was in the forest? Am I wrong about that?"

"Just taking a little side journey, Wrack. Calm down. We will find that Shadow of yours."

The mystery in her voice was not comforting, and I was certainly not prepared for what happened when Brin crashed through the brush to exit the dense woods. First there was a rush of sweet smelling air. Moss, stone, snow, and fresh crisp air danced with my senses. Something hauntingly familiar was in that smell and in the moment of quiet I had, I tried to connect it with any of my scattered and broken thoughts.

Wracked

Stepping out into the clearing was breathtaking. Grass, healthy and vibrantly green covered the large open space. Forming a perimeter around the space was the same foreboding fence of web covered trees, but at the back of it was a wall of snow covered mountains. Staring at this amazing show of untainted nature was like seeing a completely different world that lay on the other side of those trees. Taking in this sight, I somehow missed the thing in the middle of the clearing.

My eyes came down from the gleaming mountain tops and stopped on the jagged stone tip of a massive column covered in moss. Small details poking through the moss told me that this was no simple rock. Windows—some of them still containing glass but all black and lifeless—decorated the surface, and at the base was a huge door. To one side there lay the severed top of this massive broken tower. Enough of it remained intact that I could imagine how this structure would have loomed over the forest that was its neighbor.

"A day so horrible to remember. Too terrible to forget. The tower fell, the teacher died, and filled the world with nothing but regret." The words were attached to the same enchanting tune that she had been humming.

Overwhelming feelings of confusion, loss, and familiarity tore at my mind. I felt a flood of thoughts come rushing into my soul and I was helpless to stop them.

Clouds moved backwards across a dusky sky. A sound rumbled in the distance, but quickly grew closer. Just as the sound reached its peak in volume, a tower reassembled itself and jutted into the sky above.

Chapter 4

It looked old, covered in moss and discoloration from where the rain ran down its sides. Light poured out of each of the many windows in its sides. Tiny shadows could be seen in the bright windows, giving reference to how gigantic the tower was. In the area around the tower, many people were going about their daily chores. Most of them were children, all of them dressed simply. I found myself as a small child in their midst. As I walked through them, they all smiled pleasantly as I passed on my way to the forest. Before me, the trees of the forest were so alive with color and movement that it almost seemed that were singing to each other as they moved. Once free of the people around me, I fled to the forest and found myself hiding just within the edge of its embrace.

With an impossible silence, the clearing at the base of the mountain that the tower sat within was suddenly filled with armed men all clad in black and red. Some of them moved speedily into the tower itself, while others gathered up all the children into a cloud of tears and confusion. Scared and confused myself, I wanted to do something, anything to send these horrible men away. My eyes burned to signify tears were on their way, but I held them back with indignant anger.

After this strained eternity, the men emerged from the tower again behind a group of robed figures. One among them stood out, because his mere presence seemed unearthly and magical. His white hair seemed almost like a fog escaping from underneath his tiny hat. While he was their prisoner, the men gave him a wide berth, uncertain of the man's power.

The commander arrogantly strode out of his assembled men. His pointy black beard and air of command made him stand out from his men like a shiny coin tossed in with a pile of dull and tarnished buttons. He strode forward to the white haired wizard.

Wracked

From the woods, I strained to hear what they were saying. The commander kept raising his voice, while the old wizard kept his calm. There was a long silence as the commander stared at the old man. He opened his mouth, but before he could say what he was obviously drawing in the strength to utter, the wizard whispered something that had a dire effect upon the commander.

With a speed that only men who live by their sword have, the commander drew his sword and struck deep into the wizard's chest. The wizard laughed like a man who had just been released from prison, and stood even though his wound was dire. The commander withdrew his sword and stepped away from the old man, then issued an order to his men. Following the angry orders of their leader, the soldiers drew their weapons and started slaughtering everyone who stood around the wizard. The wizard remained standing, but fiddled with iron bands that were around his wrists.

At the edge of the woods I struggled with myself, caught in a storm of fear and confusion. I did not know if I should run or try to help, and in that space of my inaction my whole world was being murdered. The old wizard finally picked the lock of the iron band around his arm and then looked over at me in my hiding place. The wizard winked at me in a familiar, even joyful way, which seemed so out of place with his horrifying surroundings that I couldn't hold back the tears any longer. The muscles in my face tightened into a frown and I felt the convulsions of sobbing starting to wrack my body. Shaking my head I kept whispering, 'No no no," but my fear kept me glued to my hiding place.

A bright light escaped the one open eye of the old man and it touched me. Suddenly, everything seemed different somehow. I could hear the world better and the trees began to whisper to me. The scene before me seemed to happen in slow motion and I felt as

Chapter 4

if I were about to rush into the middle of the bloodied soldiers and make them stop, but something prevented me. It was the one word that the old man mouthed silently: "Run."

The whispering trees helped me escape slaughter, but before I was out of sight, I looked over his shoulder to see a silver light escaping the old wizard's free hand. It fell on the blood that soaked the ground of the clearing, and then back like lightning at the soldiers who were attacking the children. Everyone in the clearing started to glow until the light was so bright that it washed away everything in my vision. There was a rumbling noise and I felt a wave of force come over me that knocked me to the ground and shook the trees and the earth, then the light was gone. A sudden emptiness filled the my gut and I needed to see what had happened.

I climbed a tree—which whispered the secrets of how to climb it quickly—until I reached the very top. Looking over the green canopy, I did not see the stone guardian of the tower standing watch over the forest. But from my place in the tree I could see part of the clearing. A black orb sat amidst the twisted carnage. It seemed to unwind itself as it split into a multitude of black writhing tentacles to reveal the commander within, before it vanished into the ground at his feet. He strode over to the fallen body of the old man. His sword rose and fell. After claiming some trophy from the corpse he stormed into the woods, which silently screamed at him and seemed to somehow try and hinder him, but he took no notice.

"Beautiful eh?" Avar's voice saved me from wherever I had gone. I could see he had noticed the tears that were streaming down my face.

Wiping away the tears I mumbled, "Certainly something."

Wracked

"They say that this is really where it all began," Avar said like a child discovering that all his old stories were true. "The Cursing and all that."

"What is that song, Brin?"

"A song my father used to sing. It is beautiful and sad. Talks about the Great Tower and how when it fell all hope truly died. I love it because it reminds me of him. Never actually seen the Tower though; thought it was just a song." She paused, looking over the lush and living clearing. For a moment we all just breathed in the uncorrupted life that was there. Then Brin spoke again, "You guys ready to move?"

In Avar's eyes, I could see that he wanted to go investigate the tower, but I nodded and pulled him back towards the woods. Stumbling on his first step, he quickly adjusted back to the task at hand, and we forced our way back into the woods. This time we were heading back towards the cold heart of the woods. Feeling stone under my feet, I brushed away some of the debris to see the remains of a stone road asleep under an age-old covering. *This must have been what Brin followed to find the tower.* Curious to find other shallowly buried secrets, I observed my surroundings with greater scrutiny.

After another few days travel through the wood, we came upon strange mounds covered in vines and moss. There were just a few at first, then we came upon an area with many of them in what seemed to me like a pattern of sorts. The ground had become slightly more difficult to traverse, as it was more uneven, and there was often a dry crunching sound which escaped the occasional footfall. Something was hidden here and it called to me.

Chapter 4

My curiosity overtook my reason, and I began disturbing the vines which lay over one of these great mounds. At first I just found stone, but I continued. Soon, I found worked stone, and realized that these mounds were partially collapsed buildings. What purpose they once served or still served, I did not know.

"What the uzk are you doing?" Even in whispers, her displeasure was evident.

Suddenly ashamed I said, "I dunno, I just had to see what was underneath."

"We really shouldn't be disturbing this place." Avar chimed in, "I mean, what if there is something horrifying hiding inside?"

"You're the uzkin' Shadow Hunter," Brin mocked him. "Isn't your sworn oath to find horrifying things?"

As they argued, my fingers kept peeling away the foliage, searching for something within. It wasn't long before my curiosity was rewarded.

"I found a doorway," I said quietly, unsure if they really wanted to know.

Brin was already on edge from arguing with Avar, "You what?!"

"A door, to be exact. I think we should open it."

"Whoa!" She shouted. "You have been with us for weeks, with barely a word or opinion about anything, and suddenly now you want to open the overgrown door which lay dormant in this horrible forest for ages?"

"Yes."

"Brin's right, Wrack. I don't think we should go poking into these things."

Wracked

"Perhaps you should be less scared of the unknown, Avar. You are supposed to be fighting horrible evils, aren't you?" I was starting to sound like Brin, so much so that she chuckled. The smile that followed told me that she was ready to let me open the door.

Frustrated, Avar continued his case, "Well, I, uh. I mean. What if - I, I, I - I think we should wait a bit maybe and see if there is a—"

"A what, Avar?" I barked. "If we waited for men in black robes to hand us all the secrets, somehow I think we would be in this forest forever. Is that what you want?"

Sheepishly, he looked away. For a few moments, he had broken thoughts come to his lips, but he stopped them before he said anything and eventually surrendered to my burning desire to open that door. "Fine. We will open it, just let me pray for our protection."

"Ok."

We all sat in a circle while Avar performed a prayer ritual and burned incense. The whole time I was staring at that door, specifically at the iron handle that was the device to satisfy my urge to uncover the secrets within. Not even once did my thoughts drift to the suffering children of Yellow Liver or to Brin's life mission, nor did I have any concern for what might happen after the door was opened. Confidence that I would survive ruled my thoughts and it closed my heart to whatever praying Avar was doing.

When his muttering was finished, I sprung up with a purpose and headed towards the door. Brin grabbed my arm and I turned to her. It took all my willpower to force the scowling snarl that wanted to visit my face from making an appearance.

"What has gotten into you?" She asked softly.

Chapter 4

There was no response; I just headed for the door. Wrapping my hand around the cold iron handle, I drew in a breath and was filled with the smell of an ancient tomb, all earth, dust, and forgotten dreams. My lips curled back into a smile and I twisted the handle and I gave the door a push. Through the threshold of the door I could see nothing. It was as if there was a black curtain pulled across the frame of the door. As I breathed in the stale air from within, I was intoxicated. My eyes closed and there was a warm feeling in my throat that I had only ever felt when Brin carefully touched my ankle, before her torture had begun. Brin and Avar whispered things behind me, but they didn't register as words. When I opened my eyes again, my resolve was yet again steel and I stepped through the threshold into darkness.

Wracked

Chapter 5

Inside the hut was black as pitch. I took a step further in and put my hands in front of me to try feel around me. Behind me I heard Avar stumble in and Brin cursing before she followed us. My feet could feel the soft remains of what I hoped was a rug. Taking small steps, I forged forward. Avar bumped into me and I held him back. He started to mutter something and I shushed him before he could get much more than a sound out.

Brin finally broke the silence, "We need some uzkin' light in here."

At the utterance of the word light, some appeared. Candles on a desk ten or so paces away from us lit, seemingly by themselves. It cast flickering light into the room, but pools of shadow remained scattered and dancing around the room. Looking under me, I was walking on an old rotting carpet, old dried bones still wearing their armor and tattered remains of clothing lay strewn around the room. It looked like there had been some sort of fight in this building ages ago. A wet, squishing sound was coming from somewhere nearby. Looking back, I checked to see if I was the only one to hear it. The concentration and confusion that were on Brin and Avar's respective faces told me that I wasn't.

Wracked

Taking another careful step forward, we all moved together as one. Behind me, I heard the metal of their weapons swinging from their belts and I couldn't help but wonder why the unarmed member of our trio was in the front. Before I could crack a smile at my own misfortune, the squishing sound got a little louder until it was right in front of me. I looked down and saw a little glob of what looked like rotting flesh rolling towards us. Just after it came into view, it stopped. Brin quietly reached down for her sword and Avar let loose a tiny gasp.

The glob opened to reveal a dead, milky eye. With quick movements, it took us all in then closed and rolled its way back into the darkness. Not sure what to do next, I just stood there expecting something else to come out of the shadows. Eventually Avar couldn't take it anymore, and he blurted out, "Anyone there?!" which I am sure scored him a murderous look from Brin.

Much to our surprise a voice came back. "Might I have the pleasure of your names before I respond? You did, after all, break into my home."

Knowing that Brin would not be willing to give anything until her demands were met, I remained silent, as did she. After what seemed like an eternity of quiet, Avar couldn't take it anymore and burst forth with introductions. "I am Avar. This is Brin, and the guy in front is Wrack, as in spice rack—OW!"

"I trust, Avar, that this is not a mission where you have come to dispatch me. That would change the friendly tone our meeting has taken thus far."

Confused, Avar fidgeted behind me.

"Your armor. It rather gives away that you are one of the Silver Lady's Shadow Hunters."

"Oh. Right. No, I'm not here to kill you or anything. I— OW! Brin, quit that!"

Chapter 5

A light laugh came from the darkness up ahead. My eyes scanning the shadows found no form or figure to lock onto. The voice seemed to come from the entire space in front. Back and forth, my eyes kept moving over every bit of the flickering light trying to find purchase on any solid shape for the voice which was our host. There was a twisting sensation in my eyes and the space lost most of its color, but vision could pierce deeper into the darkness. Just past the desk where the candles sat I saw something vaguely man-shaped moving like a sheet put out on a laundry line in a lazy breeze. As if the other things were not enough to make me feel strange, that certainly did not put me at ease.

"Well then. It is a pleasure to make your acquaintance, Avar. As for your companions..." The voice drifted off for a moment. "I can tell little about you, Mistress Brin, save perhaps that you are a woman who has seen the dark underside of this world and found that it did not entirely disagree with you."

Brin gave a disapproving grunt, the way skeptics react to prophecy.

"And Wrack. Somehow I think there is little you have in common with any kind of spice rack. Long have I anticipated your arrival. How may I be of service?"

The dark form moved from standing in the back and sat in a chair near the desk. I was so focused on keeping track of this dark image, I didn't realize it had asked me a question. The last bit of pain that Brin had given Avar must have done well to keep him silent, and Brin was certainly not going to say anything to this unknown floating voice.

"You are much quieter than I expected you to be, Wrack, I must admit."

Wracked

"Some men in black robes told us to find you," Brin said before the pain wore off and allowed Avar to say something dumb. "Perhaps you can enlighten us to the reason for that."

"I see. So you don't even know why you have come to me. How odd. I expected your arrival to be full of drama, threats, demands—"

"Well, there still might be if you don't tell us why we are here." Her impatience was starting to get the better of her.

"I see. Well, with Avar's skills as a Shadow Hunter, your obvious talent with bloodshed, and the fact that you have Wrack here, you certainly have me at a disadvantage." I could see the form quietly chuckle. I felt Brin move for her sword, but I reached my hand down and gently placed it on hers. Expecting a complaint from her, I waited to do anything further; instead her hand relaxed a little, but did not leave the handle of her sword.

"You have information that I want. What must be done to convince you to give it to me?" I asked firmly.

"Ah. It seems like the great one has decided to break his silence. Unfortunately for me, I am bound to help you and so therefore I must. But I insist that you help me before payment can be fully given. Do this tiny request for me first, and you shall have that which you seek…Mister Wrack."

"What do you want?"

"A simple task that requires only basic, simple labor. This forest is strewn with the bones of heroes and villains who died in a war an age old. Spend one day collecting bones and lay them like a blanket over my hut and I shall answer your questions."

Turning away from the form for a moment, I looked at my companions. With my new sight, their flesh seemed to glow faintly in the darkness. Their eyes full of life and energy, I could see things there that usually remained hidden. Avar's objection to the task at

Chapter 5

hand was readily apparent, but his curiosity conflicted with his desire to defy this twisted request. On the other hand, something had piqued Brin's dark interest. She wanted to move forward with this task and seemed eager to do so. When our eyes first met, she did look at me oddly. I wondered if my eyes had some strange appearance when twisted into this new vision.

"We accept. One day's worth of bones for questions answers," Brin stated with an air of authority.

"Done," said the dark form. "Oh, and do be wary of the spiders."

"Spiders? Uzk," whispered Avar.

After leaving the stone hut, Brin and I quickly went to work collecting the brittle old bones that lay just under the surface of the ground. Some of the bodies still had remains of clothing or armor on them, so old that age had removed insignias and the style of armor was alien to all of us. Some bones just turned to dust at our attempt to collect them. Both Brin and Avar made sure they were wearing their gloves while working. Oddly it seemed more natural for me to collect the bones bare handed. In fact, sometimes when I touched a bone or two, I could swear they gave me a small shock that each time made me smile, a fact I did not share with my living companions.

After a short time, Brin and I had collected a decent pile of bones where Avar seemed to be like a child who was no longer hungry at the table. He kept shifting his collection around and slowly working at finding more bones in the dusty webs. Sometimes I caught him looking up at the canopy above, worried about our invisible stalkers, which he was certain were just waiting for the right moment to strike.

Wracked

One time when he was looking up, I asked him, "You still helping?" The look he returned made me certain that if I looked up I would see some eight legged giant silently descending from above. This caused me to have to look, and I saw nothing.

"Would you two stop freaking out about the spiders and get to work? Something tells me that our reward will be based on how much we collect. I will be uzk'd if you two ruin my chance at asking that uzkin' Shadow a question or two."

With the verbal lashing of our taskmaster, Avar and I returned to work. I worked my way closer to where Avar was working and tried to quietly start a conversation while we were working.

"You aren't really into this, are you?"

"Yeah. Sure. No, it's fine," he deflected.

Knowing Avar as I did, I knew all I had to say was one more thing to loosen his tongue. "Ok."

"Well, I mean. I can't help thinking about it. I am a Shadow Hunter, and he is a Shadow. Should I really be doing his bidding? Seems a little backwards to me."

"But the goal of the Hunters isn't to kill actual Shadows though. I thought you were trying to destroy the Doomed or remove the curse from the world or something."

"Yeah. We are. But how many small tasks for an obviously evil thing count against that goal? I mean, most things like him want stuff to make them more powerful. So, should I really be making my enemy more powerful when I know that someday me or some other Hunter is going to have to come back and kill it? Just seems backwards."

"Well, in my limited experience, I dunno if anything is that cut and dry. Seems like everyone and everything has his own selfish agenda. Not calling your organization selfish or anything—"

Chapter 5

"I know. I dunno. Sometimes I just think that I know a lot, but I don't know anything. Ya know?"

His words confused me for a moment. "No. I don't."

Laughing in that moment was something that came genuinely for both of us. Even though the conversation hadn't slowed us down in our work, Brin started making accusations and noises to the contrary. We quieted down and kept working for a while. When Brin moved further away from us we started talking again.

"Sure are a lot of dead things in here. What in the pit do you think happened here?" I asked him.

"Well, if you believe in legend, lots of wars and stuff happened here. The stories say that this forest used to be the home of the Elves, but I think they are just a myth. But the destruction of the tower is said to be the moment that everything was set in motion. There is a huge, long prophecy that has been told and retold and sung and stuff since before the Cursing. Looking back people, say it told everyone that the Cursing and the Doomed were foretold in the prophecy, but those kinds of things are easy to look back and say 'Oooh! We knew that was coming'. I am not sure I believe that anyone can see the future."

"What happened to the elves?"

"They all disappeared. Stories say that they were all linked to their queen and when she died or whatever that they just up and vanished. Sounds too fantastic to me."

And talking shadows, ghouls, a giant curse, and these guys called the Doomed aren't too fantastic? "What is so special about this place, that people fought over it so much?"

"Well, the trees are special and of course the tower is a place that is probably still full of ancient secrets and stuff."

"Ancient secrets?"

Wracked

"Yeah. The Great Wizard lived there more than three thousand years ago. Everyone believed at the time that he was the one who breathed magic into the world and so it was widely held that he had all kinds of magical artifacts in his tower. Somehow I doubt that the stories were accurate. Those rumors, though, were sure to send loads of people here looking for ways to fight the Doomed or save themselves when everything fell apart. Plus, I am sure that the Doomed came here too. Only way here is through these woods. Ergo, loads of dead people."

"For someone who has a goal of fighting these mythical horrors that tore apart the world, you don't seem to believe that much in some of your own stories."

Avar shrugged. "I used to believe in all of it. Just not sure what is right at the moment. Part of me thinks that I should just go in there and kill that Shadow thing."

"I don't think it is the right time for that. Call me crazy, but I think he will prove more useful alive than if we just destroyed him." I didn't have the heart to tell Avar that the Shadow had laughed at him. It was here, over the bones of long dead peoples, that I saw how much of a child still lived in Avar's heart. Someday he would have to grow up and actually become the hero that I knew he wanted to be, but right then was not the time for that.

"We better start laying these bones down on his hut before it gets dark. Unless you want to do it all yourself, Wrack." Brin shouted at us.

"Spice rack. Spicy." Avar muttered under his breath and chuckled. I couldn't help but smile at his amusement.

Bringing the piles of dusty bones back to the stone hut was more annoying than anything else. It took many trips back and forth to the piles we had made, because we had no way to create any sort of sled or other device. Occasionally I found myself picking

Chapter 5

up more bones as I crunched my way back to the hut. Once all the bones were there, we started pulling the vines away from the entire mound.

The hut was probably once a full stone house. The pile of rubble in the back significantly reduced the overall size of the actual building, a fact that remained hidden until everything was uncovered. Surprisingly there were no holes which might cast light into the part of the building that remained standing which made me believe that the whole structure may have been more than one floor before it collapsed. This would make the small hut merely the entry chamber of the old building. I tried to imagine what this area may have looked like prior to whatever cause the buildings to collapse. Try as I might, the webs and current condition of the forest were something I could not push out of my mind, and it hindered my ability to imagine this place as anything other than a ruin.

We all worked on different sides of the hut, placing the bones like a blanket over it, as the Shadow had told us. We all climbed onto the top of it and started with the roof and then placed bones in layers working our way down. Brin and I were very careful to not break any of the brittle bones. Each time a bone was placed on the building I felt it drawn and locked into position by some unseen force. Curious about this, I tried to gently remove one I had placed and found it stuck fast. Not wanting to pull too hard and possibly break the bone, I let my curiosity be satisfied that they could not be removed.

As the time wandered on, Brin and I found ourselves working next to each other. I stole glances at her face which was filled with determined concentration. The resolution that I had come to about helping her was something, I had not yet talked with her about. I thought it might be a good idea to bring it up while we were relatively alone. Still, my hesitation from the day that she seemed to want to get rid of my enigmatic presence loomed over my thoughts.

"What?"

Acting as if I hadn't heard her, I continued working.

"Out with it," she demanded.

I was flustered. "Uh. I was just thinking, I mean I was just, uh."

Out of the corner of my eye, I saw that same warm smile that was so unlike the hard exterior that she usually showed the world. Drawn in by that warmth I lost what I was about to say.

"If you don't want to tell me, that's fine. I don't need to know."

"I want to help you," the words just spilled out.

With a twinge of anger, her eyes became slits. "Help me with what?"

Taking a breath to collect my thoughts, I continued, "I know about your drive to avenge your father. You have helped me so much, I want to help you. That ok?"

"Yeah, I guess."

After a few awkward moments of working silence, she laughed a little.

"If you don't want my help, I can back off."

"Nah. It's just . . . you don't know me. Why would you want to help me? I mean, maybe if you were alive I could think of a few reasons why you might want to but—"

"Can't I just want to help you? Brin, I don't remember feeling the manner of kindness you have shown me. Ever. In my short memory most people have seen me and reacted with fear or disgust. You're different."

Chapter 5

Something I said must have been shocking. Her whole tough demeanor melted and for a brief moment I saw the woman that was hiding beneath it, a woman who was filled with longing, an overwhelming fear, and loneliness. Her eyes searched my face for any signs of lies or betrayal. "I am not that different. I am just a girl who watched her father die and her mother waste away. The people behind my father's death are probably long gone. You sure you want to get mixed up with a hopeless journey of relentless hatred at a faceless enemy?"

"Yeah. I am not doing anything else today."

She smiled, and I felt the warmth of her hand on my face for a second.

"Piece of dirt there," she said hiding behind her normal defenses again.

We worked for more hours in silence. Occasionally I caught her looking at me, sizing me up as I had seen her do with everyone else she met for the first time. It was different somehow. Part of me wished I knew what was going on in her head and hoped that she wouldn't go back to thinking I was no use to her, or worse, that I meant her harm.

It wasn't until the middle of the night that we were done placing the bones over the hut. In the darkness, I felt my eyes twist again and I saw the colorless dark world around me. The bones shimmered slightly in this new sight. Avar did not want to see the Shadow at night, so we camped a little distance away from the hut. After Avar went to sleep, Brin sat next to me.

"Your eyes look different in the dark now. You didn't drink blood or something did you?" There was a playful tone to her question that let me know that things were different between us.

"Not that you know of. How are they different?"

Wracked

"They are slitted like a cat's eyes, and they glow slightly when I look directly into them. It is kinda eerie."

"Kinda eerie? Sounds a lot eerie to me. Let's hope Avar doesn't seem 'em this way, or he might try and kill me."

There was a hush between us as things went unsaid. Until, "So, what you said earlier. Were you serious?"

"Yeah," I said. "Yeah, I was serious."

She let out a deep breath to bring even more emphasis to her eminent statement. "I don't let people in, Wrack. Avar tells me that it is because I don't want to get connected and lose them like I did my father. But something about you is so familiar, I trust you. I don't know why, but I do. So, if you wanna help me…just don't stab me in the uzkin' back."

"I don't even know how to do that."

Laughing a little she said, "Yeah, well. Maybe we should keep it that way. But seriously, right now what I am looking for is my father's sword. I think it will lead me to the people who killed him. It's a unique sword, so it is hard to hide. It even has a name: Ukumog. Not sure what that means, some old language or something. My dad said that the Silver Lady led him to the sword, and he always knew that his life was tied to it."

"How long have you been at this?"

"Since I was nine. No sign of it yet, but I am getting closer. Truth is, I think that the Doomed might have had something to do with his death."

"Why would the Doomed murder your father?"

Her face lit up with uncertainty. For whatever reason, she forgot her normal guards and answered by question. "My dad was a bard; he wandered around and sang songs and told stories for money. Avar said that he was the last of the true bards, inspired by the Silver Lady to sing the prophecy. I don't know about any of that,

Chapter 5

but the Shadow Hunters have proved useful in the past, because they think I am tied into that somehow. I just want to kill the uzker that killed my dad with his own sword."

This outpouring of truth was the largest chunk of anyone's soul that I had ever seen. The real woman that was Brin sat next to me that night. After she told me who she was, I knew I was there for a reason. It was not just coincidence that she had found me in that alley. Too much talk of this Silver Lady and the prophecy was floating around in this tangled web of events for my dark entry into their lives to be happenstance.

"We will do this together."

I don't know if it was my frank delivery of that promise or something else, but I saw a tear well up in one of her eyes, and I saw her choke it back, all things that I don't know if I would have caught if not for my new dark sight. The rest of the night we sat in silence and she went to sleep right next to me, rather than at least a sword distance as she normally did.

When the morning came, Avar seemed more prepared to see the Shadow. There was still conflict in him about this whole situation, but I doubted that he would do something dumb like try and kill it. After our normal morning business, we found our way back to the stone hut which now was exposed and covered in bones. It looked very strange in the daylight to see the blanket of bones over the dark stone. I wondered how long it would take the hut to again be covered in dust and vines. The door was open and the dark curtain of shadow was still across it.

"I think I will wait out here."

"Okay, Avar," I said. "If there is any trouble, just come inside."

Avar nodded to me, and Brin and I crossed the dark threshold into the Shadow's lair.

Wracked

"Ah, my busy, busy friends. You have done a wonderful job on my home. I thank you."

My eyes twisted again in the darkness and I could see the outline of a man sitting in the chair. His form much more distinct than before, and I could feel his presence had grown considerably since our last visit.

Brin was impatient, "Ok. You have your uzkin' bones, now give us information."

"In a hurry, my dear? Your goals are closer than I you might wish to believe."

"What? What do you know about me?"

"I know where you might find your father's sword."

"Might?" I asked.

"Turn of phrase, Mister Wrack. I do know where the sword Ukumog is, at this very moment."

Excitement leapt off Brin's body like lightning. "Where? Tell me where it is!"

"Patience. Patience my dark haired angel of vengeance. The task was for Wrack, and it is his question to ask."

Even without turning, I could feel Brin's stare fall on me. In light of my promise the night before, I felt I had no choice but let the price of our labor answer this question. "Where is the sword?"

"I thought you might ask me that, Mister Wrack. Let's see. Due east of my home there is a path out of the woods. It is a little overgrown and such, but it will lead you to the south. There is a cliff to the south west of Yellow Liver, and there you will find a cluster of trees. Within the trees you will find a shack. The sword is currently claimed by the one who calls that shack home."

"That's it?" Brin was hoping for more. She pressed him for further details, "Who is inside?"

Chapter 5

"Indeed. That is it. You will meet the inhabitant soon enough. If you find yourself again lost, come find me. I am sure I can give you more work in exchange. Unless you would like to ask the Doomed about your father? I am sure they would give some interesting answers."

The sinister smile which was beaming from the Shadow was one I did not need to see to know was there. He was definitely not telling us everything. After he was silent for a moment, Brin stepped out through the doorway. Before I could follow her, I felt the Shadow draw close to me and he whispered, "You are at a crux at this moment, Wrack. A space where you have the freedom to choose several different paths. I thought I saw it before, but your return has sealed my understanding."

"Who am I?"

Stunned silence hung for a moment. "Deeper still is my understanding. I could tell you more, but to do so would taint your choices. It might force you to become who you were. Is that something you want?"

My mind flooded with painful bloody images and memories of revelry in pain and death. "No. I think I will see where this path leads me."

"Well, if you change your mind, return to me. If my prices are too high, you can always seek out the master of Yellow Liver. He will know you." After a brief pause he continued, "Their fates are now tied to yours," he indicated my friends who were waiting outside, "but you know that already, of course. Farewell, Wrack. I am sure we will meet again. Though, not too soon I hope. Careful of the spiders on your way out."

I searched the form next to me for a face. Frustrated that I could not read the voice which was taunting me, I felt an anger growing inside me. I wanted to grasp the Shadow and devour it,

Wracked

to slaughter and twist that which tormented me. The smell of the smoke from a fresh fire filled my noise and I choked back a bitter hatred in my throat. *I knew this taunting voice, but from where? Was it a dream or were all my dreams fragments of my memories. Just who was I anyway?*

"One more thing will I give you, Wrack." The harsh cold of his presence licked at the back of my neck as he whispered to me. "There is a prisoner that only you can set free. Break the prison and let them out. You will think you have found the prisoner many times before the true one is found. Not easily will they be released. Now go. Our time is done for now. We will see each other again."

The biting words, but soothing voice of the Shadow forced me back to my senses. "Until then, Shadow."

Stepping out into the daylight, I met my companions and we set off through the woods. Brin was moving faster than before, cutting around trees and brush as if there was someone in danger that she had to save. Many times Avar and I fell behind, and she made us feel guilty for keeping her from her goal. It was only because of Avar's incessant complaining about being tired that Brin was even willing to stop for the night. The pure fuel of revenge was willing to burn her alive just to see one real milestone towards her greater goal. I wondered if she would change if she found the sword, if she would become even more driven to destroy anything she thought was connected with her father's death.

Avar slept, but Brin tossed and turned. When she woke to see me watching her, she gave me an accusatory look. Moments later she moved her sleeping spot over next to me without either of us saying a word. As she was falling asleep the quiet words "Thank you" escaped her. Gently, I brushed the dark curls away from her face. Her hair was soft and silky, yet thick and strong. This contradiction seemed to fit the woman it grew from well.

Chapter 5

Sitting in the silence, I was a guardian over my two friends. I felt different. When we came into this wood, I was simply a tag-along. Now I felt like true companion to them both. I dreaded the next time our small band found ourselves in a fight. Useless was something I no longer wished to consider myself.

A clicking noise brought me out of my thoughts and I looked above me to see where it had come from. My eyes, twisting with dark sight, locked with eight eyes attached to a spider the size of a horse, hanging inches over my head. Calmly, I watched its mandibles cleaning themselves, and it slid even closer to me. Its eyes were riddled with an ancient wisdom that I could not understand. Transfixed by seeing the light of my own eyes reflected in its black orbs I did nothing as it slowly drew even closer.

Light filled all eight of the black orbs and in each one I saw the image of a woman. Beautiful and sad, the woman stood alone covered from head to toe in layers of lace made from wispy webs. When her eyes looked up and met mine, she was suddenly gone and was replaced by a purple gem affixed into something. As the image widened, I saw that it was the most brilliant amethyst gemstone which sat atop a silvery scepter. Holding this scepter was a skeletal hand, the bones of the hand were red and dripping with bloody ichor. The fist clenched the scepter and the image were gone. The spidery messenger seemed to nod at me, and with as much quiet as it had arrived, it climbed back into the canopy, where I saw many many others all watching over us.

There was a yelp of a wolf nearby, and later I saw dark forms ascending to the canopy near where the sound came from. My friends slept peacefully and unaware of our secret friends. In the morning, the spiders were gone and we forged our way through the rest of the wood. Until we left the wood, I knew I was not the only one watching over us, for I occasionally caught glimpse of a skittering shadow cast from above.

Out into the wilds again, Brin continued her breakneck speed over the yellow rocky terrain towards the shack which held the secret to her struggle. Days seemed to rush by as we struggled through the rough ground and avoided any other contact with people, as it might "slow us down". I thought that the pace we were moving might kill Avar, until one night Brin came back from hunting with a smile beaming from her face.

"Rest tonight my friends, tomorrow I reclaim my father's blade."

CHAPTER 6

When daybreak came Brin was up and ready to go long before Avar even began to stir. She spent the time practicing with her sword and checking to make sure all her knives were secure on her boots and the back of her belt. Her ability to wait ran thin, and eventually she was lightly kicking Avar to get him moving. She was so impatient that she even had breakfast ready before she woke him. Cooking up until then had always been Avar's job. It might actually have been the smell of the food that got Avar out of bed; at the very least it was more persuasive than Brin's boots.

After Avar prepared himself for the day, and got suited in his mantle of armor, we headed out after the elusive shack. Brin made us travel light, so most of their camping supplies and packs were left hidden in a cache near where we had made camp. I had nothing to hide.

Moving through the hills leading to the cliff was easier than traversing the forest. Brin seemed like she really knew where we were going this time, not like the winging it without telling us that she probably did in the forest. "Last night I made a trail for myself coming back to you guys. When I saw the shack, I almost went in alone. Hopefully my waiting won't come back to bite me."

Wracked

With as eager as Brin had been acting about getting her father's sword back, neither Avar or I were surprised at her statement. We followed the trail for an hour or so and then Brin stopped. We could see the cliff from there, but there was no shack. Avar tried to ask her a question and she told him to shut his mouth very rapidly, a good sign that something had gone wrong. The next few hours had us following the trail back and forth and Brin getting angrier with each passing moment. The search widened a bit, letting us see parts of the cliff, woods, and surrounding hills that we hadn't traveled before. My feet never got tired or hurt, so I couldn't sympathize with Avar when he started complaining about all the back and forth. Brin did not want to hear it.

Around midday we stopped so that Avar could rest his feet, and so he and Brin could have a light meal. Brin was seething with a bitter anger than she could not find the shack again. After a long silence mixed with Avar's usual eating noises, I saw Brin's lips start to move as if she were talking to herself.

"We will find it," I attempted to ease her mind.

"Oh, we will find it alright. I don't care if I have to burn down the uzkin' woods to find the uzkin' shack, we will uzkin' find it."

There was no correct response to the level of frustration and anger that exploded from Brin. I just shut my mouth and gave a fake smile so that she would stop yelling. A few more moments of Avar munching away at his food went by and then Brin exploded again.

"Uzk! I swear to you, I saw the uzkin' place last night! How the uzk—" She stopped speaking, drew her sword and whirled around.

Chapter 6

Avar grabbed for his mace and stood up, dropping the rest of his lunch on the ground. Leaning sideways where I sat was the only thing I could think to do to see what they were looking at. There was a man in a black and red robe standing just at the edge of our camp holding a armload of twigs, plants, and other foliage. No one moved for a heartbeat or two and, then the man threw down his collection and darted off into the brush.

"Come back here!" Brin screamed reflexively then took off in pursuit. Avar looked at me as if to ask me what to do and then himself ran after her. I found myself with little choice but to follow.

Darting through the terrain, I watched the race from behind, first a flutter of a robe then a streak of raven colored hair, followed by the glimmer of runic armor, then the leader changed direction and I heard something fly at high speed through the air. Then another object cut through the air. This time the object found a mark as a man's voice gave a small cry of pain. I was certain that the voice was not Avar's. Fractions of a moment later, there was a loud cracking noise like a tree had just been snapped in half accompanied by a flash of light. I heard Brin shout something and Avar respond.

I pressed myself against a tree and looked around to see what was going on. Avar and Brin were likewise hiding and she mouthed words to Avar, who nodded in response. There was no sign of the robed man. Uncertain what I should do, I remained behind the tree and waited.

Eventually Brin and Avar stealthily found me, and we three retreated back to Avar's ruined lunch. "That was the same figure that I saw at the shack last night. I think I wounded him, so we will let him think he got away and then follow the blood."

"Did you see that guy? I think he threw lightning at me or something!"

95

Wracked

"First run in with a wizard, Avar?" Brin asked, sarcastically.

"Am I that obvious?"

Brin laughed, "In more ways than just that. Just be glad you aren't all jaded like me."

After finishing his food and resting for a bit, Avar was finally ready to move just as the sun was about to touch the horizon. Brin insisted that we move the hidden gear just in case. By the time we got back to trying to find the shack it was nearly dark. Creeping through the woods, Brin made Avar and his shiny armor stay a good distance behind her. It wasn't long before she was on the trail. Leaves on the plants and patches of dirt on the ground, all touched with dark red drops. Looking over her shoulder to see if we were behind her, she beamed with delight.

Ahead of me, I saw Brin hunker down and wave her hand for Avar and me to do the same. Try as I might, I couldn't see what she was so focused on so I tried to listen. I listened to the slight breeze nudging its way through the crowd of brown leaves and empty branches. The dead and dying leaves rustled under the force of the air. Beyond the breeze, I heard a distant roar. A familiar roar. My mind pictured the falls that were the first sounds I heard other than my own screams of pain. *How bizarre that I would end up in nearly the same place as where I began?* Then I heard it. A slight humming, like that of a child out to play all alone. "What do you see?" I whispered over to Brin.

First she put her finger to her lips, then after a few glances at something she looked back at me. "I think it is a little gnome or something."

"Gnome?" I asked.

"Gnomes are just a story from the north, they aren't real," came Avar's whispered contribution.

Chapter 6

"Well, that one is real enough, and it is cleaning up the trail. We are gunna have to follow it," Brin insisted.

The three of us sat in silence. Brin was the only one that could see the thing, while I sat near her listening to the strange disjointed song that it was humming to itself. The noise seemed dry and hollow with very little actual life. Eventually it started drifting away from us. Brin was extra careful and let the gnome get almost out sight before she started following it, making sure to keep Avar and his noisy armor in the back.

The distant roar of the falls grew louder as we left the cover the trees and brush and came out onto the open cliff. On the edge of the cliff, looking like it was about to fall down, was a shack made of mismatched wood, stone, and scraps of tin. The tiny figure went in through the front door. We waited for a light to come on inside the building, but none came.

"It can't be big enough for more than one or two rooms."

"Very astute, Avar. You wanna go knock on the door and ask politely for the sword?"

"If that would work, then yeah."

"We are going to have to wait until it gets dark, otherwise we risk being seen from the windows."

I felt like a predator stalking its prey, waiting for cover and condition to be just right before the strike, lingering on the edge of our camouflage before risking a charge out into the open. Avar shivered a bit from the wind up there near the cliff. I couldn't even feel the cold.

As the blanket of night was fully pulled over our heads, I felt my senses grow sharper. It was as if the noise of the day and the haze of the light were obstacles preventing me from experiencing the world around me clearly. The smell of the wet falls drifted into my lungs. It felt a little like the home I never wanted to return to.

Wracked

Brin crept up toward the house and listened for activity. Shortly thereafter, she stood up by the front door and waved us over. As I moved towards her, I saw the dark horizon beyond the cliff. In the distance, I saw twinkling points of light both above and below. My mind briefly wandered to the camps or homes of strangers that lay scattered about the horizon. How many of them lived in fear and what were the reasons for it? I wondered where that bloody skeleton holding the scepter was, and why I hadn't mentioned it to Avar yet. *One thing at a time, I suppose.*

Avar and Brin got to work examining the doorway, dusting it gently and carefully looking at the ground in front of it. I watched them from a short distance away, not entirely sure what they were doing.

"What are you doing?" I couldn't help but ask.

"Looking for traps or eyes." Such confidence in Avar's voice, I almost forgot that he was new at this.

Brin gave a mocking laugh. "Ever kicked in a door Avar?"

"Yeah. Dreyan showed me how to do it."

"But have you ever actually done it, like on a hunt?"

"Uh. Well. Um." His voice trailed off.

"I'll take that as a no."

Brin reached down and grabbed some dirt and mixed it with some spit then smeared it over a spot on the doorframe. Avar looked at her confusedly. "Coulda just been a knot in the wood or it could be a spy hole. A little mud does the job nicely," she answered his unspoken question. "You see anything over there?"

"Nope. I think we are all clear. For a wizard, he doesn't protect his home very well."

"Those are always the ones that worry me." She paused and a smirk developed on her face. "You wanna kick in the door?"

"Me? I dunno. I might knock over the whole shack."

Chapter 6

"What, are you scared? Aw. Little Hunter all scared by the crazy man in the shack."

"The crazy WIZARD that throws LIGHTNING, and I am not scared. I just don't want to push the shack off the cliff."

"Uh huh. It's ok, greenie. I won't tell Wrack that this is your first time."

Avar made a face at Brin when she turned away from him and stood up.

"Watch closely, Avar. You get to do this next time." Without any further explanation, she swiftly kicked the door, and it flew open from the force of her expertise. The entire building shook and swayed a bit. Weapon drawn, she didn't wait to see if the building would fall, she just walked in.

"I coulda done that," Avar muttered as he drew his mace and followed her in.

I waited until the building stopped shuddering from the attack, then I went in after them.

It was nearly empty on the inside of the building. One door on the opposite wall, a small table, a chair, and an old cot that looked like no one had slept in it for a long time. Brin was slowly walking across the protesting floorboards in an effort to ease their complaining. Avar's eyes examined every inch of the area near the bed. I carefully stepped over near the table. BAM! She had kicked open the other door in the room.

"UZK! Just a uzkin' empty pantry. Where the uzk could they have gone? Uzkin' wizards."

"Two doors kicked in. They know we are here now for sure."

"Avar, there is ONLY ONE ROOM!"

"Uh, maybe there isn't." I calmly interrupted their argument.

Wracked

"You see something?"

She was right. I wasn't sure if it were visible to them, but there was a tiny leak of flickering light escaping from some of the floorboards near the cot. I pointed them out to Brin who immediately grabbed the dagger from her belt and started prying open the door that lay hidden there. With a short few attempts she popped open the door to reveal a spiral stone stair carved out of the cliff below the shack.

Brin let loose a tiny gasp of excitement and started her careful descent into the dimly lit steps below. Avar followed with me closely behind. The light reflecting on the stone was coming from far below; the smoothly carved stone was nearly reflective even with the low light. As we slowly descended, eventually I was even able to see a reflection of my own eyes in the stone. Brin's description was correct: catlike slits with a dim twisting light coming from within.

A sudden stop pulled me out of my vain musings. We had reached the bottom of the stairs. From the room I could hear two distinct voices, one deeper that spoke with some authority and the other was a cowering scratchy voice.

"No, bring me the sulfur. Yes, that's the one."

Tapping Avar on the shoulder, I motioned silently to ask if he or Brin could see up ahead. It took a few attempts to get through to Avar and he shook his head.

"You need to fix the circle over there. Draw it more like mine here, see? Those noises up there must have been them. You are sure you were not followed?"

"I'z cleaned up the blood as master wantsed."

"Won't be long before they find the door. They might have friends with them." I heard him suck air through his teeth as man bitten by a sharp pain.

Chapter 6

"Master need help?"

"Yes. Finish the circle here, Jugless. Good, now fetch me the bundle."

Brin slowly leaned into the light coming from the room. Her eyes grew wide and she whispered, "They are trying to open a doorway. We have to act now!" With that, she charged into the room.

I came around the corner just in time to see the robed figure in the middle of the room look at Brin, then the gnomish figure carrying a long bundle wrapped in cloth. The wizard drove a silver knife into his own hand and dripped the blood wildly in a circle around himself. Brin charged in vain at the man, for when he was done making the circle, he vanished. The very moment before he vanished our eyes met, and an odd smile spread across his face.

Wind rushed to the center of the room and then back outward, knocking us and many things in the magical laboratory over. Glass shattered, pages turned, and fluids spilled. Leaping to her feet, Brin chased over to the hooded gnomish figure, who was trying to escape with a bundle that was more than three times its size. With winded ease, she caught up to it and grabbed at the bundle, throwing it and the gnome back into the room. It wasn't until colliding with the floor that the gnome and its parcel were separated.

"Please don't kill! Jugless can no hurt fierce lady and her powerful friends!" It groveled on the floor.

The bundle was not just some roll of cloth. The weight of it was obvious as Brin lifted it off the floor. Avar started looking over the room, searching between bookshelves, desks, shelves, and work tables. Jugless' eyes traveled from Avar to me where they seemed to rest for a painfully pathetic moment. He looked down at my hand, which started to hurt, and when my gaze followed, I found that

Wracked

some piece of broken glass had cut open my hand in the blast. The true sting of pain came after I noticed the wound and pulled the fragment of glass out of my hand.

Slowly and carefully, Brin started to untie the bundle that lay before her. While we were all distracted, Jugless apparently tried to make an escape because I heard sliding steel as Brin's sword was loosed from its resting place and found its point an inch away from Jugless' neck. "Me sorry! Me Sorry! Me try no to escape again!"

She looked at him with utter disgust and turned back to her prize. Jugless could not have been more than a foot tall and his deformed features made him look more like a partially melted wax doll than what I suppose I thought a gnome should look like.

"I don't see a sword here, Brin."

"Its ok, Avar, I think I have it here."

With shaking, but careful hands, Brin slowly peeled back the wrapping of the bundle. I felt the room grow slightly colder as the blade came into view. Tears formed in her eyes as she looked over the only concrete piece of her father she still knew existed.

It was as long as a sword should be when wielded in one hand. The blade itself was flat and black, wider than that of a normal sword, and it didn't taper as it came to the end which didn't come to a point as most blades do. Its point was squared, making the blade itself a kind of black rectangle. The tapered edges of the blade where it had been sharpened were strikingly silver in comparison to the rest of the metal. There was no real hilt, save for a tiny hook that would allow it to catch onto a ring which was attached to a belt that lay there with the blade. The handle was bound to the blade by dark red leather straps and was entirely made out of a bone. From the looks of it, the bone looked like a human leg bone, but it was hard to tell. As if all this were not strange enough, a collection of faintly glowing symbols floated next to the flat of the blade. They

Chapter 6

were so dim it was if they were barely noticeable. The appearance of such a macabre sword and the idea that it was tied to Brin's father made me wonder what sort of man this bard might have been.

She reached forward and picked up the blade which separated from the ring with a distinctive *clink!* She raised the blade to her eyes and drank in every detail of it. Running her fingers over its smooth, deadly surface, it seemed for a moment as if she might actually bring it to her lips and kiss it. The shuffling noise of Jugless' anxiety pulled her back to us before any such embrace could have happened.

Brin smiled, "Avar. Wrack. Meet my father's sword. Meet Ukumog."

Her attention was paused on the blade for only a moment more before she turned to the pitiful frightened creature kneeling a few feet away. She set the sword back on the table and started wrapping Ukumog's belt around her waist, stopping only for a second to slap Avar's hand as he reached out towards one of the glowing runes.

"Who is your master?" Her voice was brutal and cold.

"Please no hurt me! Jugless am useful! Jugless am good!"

"Blah blah blah. Who is your master?"

"I would answer her questions if I were you." Avar tried to help.

The little creature paused for a moment as if it were weighing its options. "Master am a wizard. Him far away from here now. You no can gets him."

"Oh, yeah? That some kind of challenge? What is your master's name, little gnome?"

"He isn't a gnome," Avar said matter-of-factly.

The coldness of Brin's questioning stare made Avar finish the thought without her having to say a word.

Avar's eyes grew wide for a second. "Uh. He is a Hemodan, not a gnome."

Looking back at the creature I searched its melted face and saw that it was a tiny wax mask. Brin must have seen the same thing because she pointed her old sword and indicated that Jugless should remove it. Small gloved hands pushed back the hood and revealed an obviously poorly crafted wax mask with glass eyes.

"What is a Hemodan?" I whispered to Avar.

"A magical construct made out of dirt and wizard's blood."

The mask left behind a dark red clumpy and slightly wet face with dents for eyes and mouth. It frowned up at Brin with hollow eye sockets and placed the mask on the floor.

"What is your Master's name?"

Jugless remained in a panicked silence. His sockets flitting over all three of us.

"We should just kill the horrible little thing. He and his master share thoughts and feelings."

"And feelings?" Brin's question was loaded with malice.

"Uh, yeah."

Grabbing Jugless by the neck, Brin scooped him off the ground and slammed his little scab-like body down on the table next to Ukumog. I winced and felt bad for the little creature which was whimpering in pain.

"So, your master can feel that? Eh?"

"Y-yes. Him can feel it," Jugless managed to say between pained struggling sounds.

"What is his name? What is his name? What is his name!"

My mind flashed back to memories of the children outside the wall, pinned helplessly in the clutches of those grey skinned nightmares. I knew that Brin was just using her brutal wiles to coax

Chapter 6

information from Jugless, but there was a malice that lay behind her eyes that didn't seem normal. More disturbing was Avar's calm acceptance of the activity that was happening in front of him.

"Grumth! Him name am Grumth! Please no hurt me!"

"Grumth. Ok. Whom does he work for? One of the Doomed?"

The whining and struggling stopped and Jugless stared in shock at Brin. Those dark red sockets were filled with fear and anticipation. "Jugless not know what you talking about. What Doomed?"

Brin laughed and tightened her grasp around Jugless' throat. "THE Doomed. Don't play games with me. I know about wizards and how their power is tied to the Doomed. So, either your master is some hold out from an ancient time of legend or he is a minion of the Doomed. Which is it?"

His choking actually sounded like he was trying to let loose a slight giggle. "My master am tricky. Him have two powers fooled."

"Playing with the Doomed? Your master must be good if he can do that." Avar seemed genuinely impressed.

A smile appeared at the compliment. "Yes. Master is a genius."

"My master is so amazing. My master is smarter than the doomed," Brin mocked Jugless, which then became anger. She slammed him on the table again and choked him harder. "What's his game? Where did he get this sword?"

Laughter leaked out of its tiny wound of a mouth. Frustrated and angry Brin's face turned to rage and with a blur of action there was suddenly a tiny glove laying on the floor and a screaming captive squirming in her grasp. "Did your master feel that? Did that feel good? Because it felt uzkin' great to me!"

105

Wracked

Avar tensed and opened his mouth but no words came out. The rage on Brin's face hadn't dissipated and I was concerned that she was going to continue chopping off bits of the little creature. I moved in and put my hand on her sword arm. "Brin."

"What?!"

"We aren't going to get anything this way. You need to think clearly here. I need you to think clearly."

The rage slowly drained from her face and she looked in disgust at Jugless. She choked him one last time and then let go of him. Stepping up to the table where she had been, I said calmly, "Jugless. Please tell us what your master is up to. We need to know."

"Him in Skullspill."

"Skullspill? The Baron's city?" asked Avar.

"Yes. Him work for da red liche."

"Oh uzk." Worry in Avar's tone made me worry.

"What is his plan? You said he had two powers fooled?" Brin continued her assault.

Jugless gave a smart little laugh. "Yes. Him workin' with Plague Master, too. Dem not know he workin' wit da other."

"He is pitting two of the Doomed against each other? For the love of the Lady. Are you sure?"

"Yes. Yellow Liver am gunna be in trouble!" Jugless giggled like a child that has a secret, and it shot worry directly into my heart.

Avar was instantly concerned, "What? What is going to happen to Yellow Liver?"

A knowing grin spread across his viscous face. "Not know everything, but Captain of Guard do. Master make sure that the city not ready for when Plague Master show up." He giggled.

"Uzk." Avar backed away from the table and started pacing.

Chapter 6

"Is he saying what I think he is saying, Avar?" Brin's rage was starting to return.

"If you are thinking that one of the Doomed is going to attack Yellow Liver, then yeah."

"What does this have to do with my father? I have my sword, uzk that town anyway."

"Well, if Grumth works for the Doomed, it might be that they know more about the sword. Looks like your theory about the Doomed being involved in your father's death might be right."

The rage subsided and a look of relief came over her face. Briefly a smile appeared as she looked across the room at Ukumog sitting on the table. "We need to get moving then. Skullspill is weeks away on foot." She said as she walked across the room and collected the blade from the table.

"What about Yellow Liver?" I asked with enough power that they all looked at me. "We can't just let this madman's game unfold. Plus, if this Captain knew Grumth, he might know more about the sword. We should check on that while we are close."

Brin paused to think for a moment and attached Ukumog to her belt with that distinct *clink!* "You're right. We should see what he knows. But I don't want to get caught there in the middle of a war."

My silence was taken as agreement, but some part of me wanted to see one of these Doomed up close and personal.

"You cannot stop master's plan! Yellow Liver will fall! Jugless can no let you—" with a *clink* and a whirl the Hemodan was severed at the waist where he had climbed to his feet on the table. The runes on the blade glowed stronger for a moment as the killing blow was delivered and I, too, felt a slight tingle just under my skin at watching Ukumog in use for the first time. The feeling of death hung in the room. That sword frightened me.

Wracked

"Right, he fed his master enough of our plans. Let's go."

Avar followed Brin up the stairs. I lingered in the room for only long enough to collect the tiny hood and wax mask before I left. Something told me there were more answers there, but Brin's impatience was not to be tested, so I left the secrets behind like old friends that I never had the chance to meet.

Chapter 7

Traveling under the night sky I found very relaxing, as opposed to having the burning sun beating down on us. Our progress was somewhat slowed by Avar and Brin's lack of dark sight. As Brin grew tired, I would have to keep an eye on the terrain ahead to make sure she didn't accidentally lead us off a cliff. We found the stashed gear and started making our way back to Yellow Liver. Not long after did we have to make camp, however.

Brin slept away from me again, with Ukumog right next to her. I couldn't help but feel a little like I had been replaced. I knew I couldn't compete with the memory of her father. It had been her driving force for a long time. Still, there was something very scary about the blade to me. There were times in the night when I found myself staring at the blade and a desire grew to want to touch it. My lingering fear of it kept my desire at bay.

Morning came and with it brought the painful light of the sun. It seemed even more oppressive than usual. *Maybe I am finally growing tired.* A whisper inside my mind thought of the comfortable soil of my grave and the idea of sleep was quickly escorted from my thoughts. *If I sleep, will I ever wake again?* Perhaps this was the great secret to my dark immortality. I tried to move my mind to other things, and as we continued our journey, I danced with the vision that the spider had given me in the forest.

Wracked

"So, what exactly is our plan?" Avar's comment invaded my thoughts.

"Uh, good question. Brin, what do you think?" I asked.

Winded from cutting through some brush, she wiped some sweat off her brow. "Dunno yet. Haven't really thought much about it. Part of me thinks we should just skip on to Skullspill."

"I would hate to miss on the chance to get information from the Captain, though," I lied.

"Yeah, I guess," she paused. "The idea of getting caught in some uzkin' war between overzealous minions of the Doomed kinda makes me wonder if it is a good idea though."

"I am sure it will be worth it," Avar said.

After a day or two traveling we came up to the wall of Yellow Liver, back at the same entrance that I first came through.

"They might still be looking for us."

"Uzk, Avar. It has been like a month since we left. I am sure there are more important things on their minds."

"I dunno. Ghouls attacking Spicy and stuff. I think we made more of an impression than we usually do."

"Oh yeah, I forgot about that," Brin muttered.

Reflexively I rubbed the spot on my side where I had been stabbed. What did that creature do with that talon?

Brin's brow furrowed and she asked, "Spicy? What the uzk is with that?"

"You know. Wrack. Spice Rack. Spicy."

"Whatever." Brin was about as amused with the nickname as I was.

As we got closer to the gate, I noticed some familiar faces among the people living in the shacks and tents outside the wall. I scanned the crowd for the boy with no luck.

Chapter 7

"Yeech. It stinks out here. These people need to do something about that."

"They are uzkin' homeless, Avar. They can't even get into the city to find work. Not the best way to live, but I don't think they have much choice." Brin's defense of these downtrodden people surprised me.

"Yeah. Sorry, I guess."

Closer still we drew to the city. We had joined the line to go through the gate. Avar pointed to a piece of parchment posted up next to the gate. From this distance all we could see was NOTICE written in big bold letters and a face below that looked like me.

"Oh, uzk. I don't want to get into a fight with a guard to get in again. That is what started all that mess with those other two."

"Let's step off to the side. Maybe we can slip in after dark," I suggested

Avar smiled, "Good plan. They certainly won't be looking for some half dead guy trying to sneak in after dark."

"Will be easier to do at night than in broad daylight. I spent sometime with the people out here before I went in the city. Maybe they will have some ideas."

"Fine, but no complaining about the stink, Avar." Brin was still in no mood for Avar's whining.

"I just said one thing! Don't tell me you weren't thinking it too."

"I wasn't," said Brin.

We slipped out of the line and made our way over to the shacks and tents off to the side. I was silently greeted by every face in the cloud of dirty people. One old woman waved us over to her hovel. Following the invitation we all went in, even Avar. She looked both happy and sad at me as she said, "They took him. My grandson. They just hopped over the wall and took him."

Wracked

There were a few moments of denial when I didn't connect to her words. Then it hit me, the brave boy. My eyes grew wide as my mind and mouth fought over which words to let escape. Finally, "What? Who? The ghouls? When?" came out.

"Two nights ago." She started to weep. "He used to tell me that you were here to save us. After you left he told everyone that you were going to save us. Are you going to save us? Save him?"

I was at a loss. There was a desire to say something comforting, but I did not want to fill this poor woman with empty hope. Our plans had nothing to do with saving her grandson and I did not know if I could talk Brin into trying, especially if the ghouls had one of the Doomed as their master.

Walking over to the woman, Avar placed his hand on her shoulder and said with genuine compassion, "We will do what we can to save him." It seemed to comfort the woman for the small time that lived between that and when Brin tapped Avar angrily on the shoulder.

"Are you uzkin' mad?" She whispered accidentally loud enough for everyone in the shanty town to hear her. "We are not chasing some kid into the maw of the Doomed." Turning to the old woman, "I am sorry, but your grandson is probably gone. We have bigger things afoot than saving one boy."

The woman tried to hold back the waves of sorrow and nodded to Brin. She then turned from us and waved us out of her hovel.

Once outside Avar could not stop himself. "Way to go Brin." Seeing him angry for the first time was not what I expected. He was calm, but furious and even more animated with his expression and limbs. Hands flying around in every direction to assert his point. I wondered if this was the first time that Avar had actually stood up to her. "I know you think that vengeance for your

Chapter 7

father is more important than anything else, but what you fail to see is that this is all tied together! Them, us, the Doomed, everything! Even if you don't believe in the prophesy, you are a uzkin' part of it! Like it or not!" With a flurry of pages from his book as he turned to an earmarked page and began reading,

> 'Storyteller's daughter filled with rage.
> Black blood from another age.
> Two combined.
> One to find.
> Death and light left behind.'

"That's you! Like it or not!"

"Uzk you and your uzkin' prophesy!" She shouted.

Avar continued to argue, "Those are your FATHER'S words Brin! He wrote them, not me, not the order, not the Lady. It was the last of the storytellers. Your father!"

Anger and tears radiated from her face, and she stormed off deeper into the honeycomb of hovels.

"So, I guess we wait for her to cool off?" My words hit a wall of silence. "Is that really part of the Prophesy?"

"Yeah. It is really long. That one piece, Garrett from the order made sure I had written down. I can only remember bits and pieces of it."

"You really think it is her job to fight the Doomed?"

He let loose a defeated chuckle. "Doesn't matter. I don't think she cares. But we can't ignore what's happening here."

"What if there is a Doomed here? We don't have the power to fight one of them? Do we?"

Again my words caused silence. He looked at me and I saw a sad realization in his eyes.

113

Wracked

"There is a Doomed here isn't there?" I asked.

"Yeah. I think so. The Ghoul. He is bound to the Baron. Garrett told me he uses this city as his personal feeding ground. Told me to ignore it, but I just can't."

"Ok. We will find a way to help them, Avar." I paused for a moment, but my curiosity got the best of me, "Who is Garrett?"

"High ranking Hunter. He was my teacher. And my father. Pretty much in that order of priority. We should find Brin and get into the city before they close the gate for the night.

Shocking how quickly it got dark. It seemed that summer was coming to an end and we were sliding into autumn. In my bones I could feel that it would be a cold one.

It wasn't hard to find Brin in the midst of the unfortunate people in the honeycomb of hopelessness. They all gave her a wide berth as she paced in a circle muttering to herself. Before we got too close everyone heard her yell ". . . uzkin' Avar!"

"Maybe you should go get her. I don't want to stir her up anymore than she is."

"Good idea."

Weaving through the crowd that had gathered around her, I quickly found myself in the center with her. Ukumog was plunged into the ground near and she seemed to be talking at it. I couldn't tell if the people watching her were scared, entertained, or concerned. Their blank faces were impossible to read, and when I stepped into the middle it was almost as if they were just shadows looming on the outside of the scene. Before I could speak, I found myself starring at the blade again. It felt like I was expecting it to say something to me, and I was afraid to go any closer to Brin or to it.

"What?!" She shouted at me.

"You ok?"

Chapter 7

"Yeah! I am uzkin' great! What makes you ask such a stupid question?!"

I tried to let her rage just wash over me, "Is the yelling really necessary?"

"I dunno! Why don't you ask Avar if it is written in his uzkin' book?!"

"Brin, prophesy be damned. You gotta do what you think is right. Don't let Avar and his book push you around." At the mention of the word prophesy there was whispering that came from the crowd around us.

"Well, what the uzk is right then? We can't do what he wants us to, Wrack. It's uzkin' suicide."

"Is that really what is wrong?"

She hesitated to respond and gave me a guilty look. "What about my father? If we run off on some suicide mission, who avenges him? Hrm?"

"From everything I have heard, your father was a brave man. What would he want you to do?"

The anger in her face relaxed and her thoughts drew within. Looking at the blade a tearful smile leapt to her face and she let fly a haunting song from her lips.

'Shadows rise and shadows fall
One shadow forged to kill them all
From haughty tower
To sunken grave
We know their names

Wracked
Hungry for each other's strength
Tearing ripping at the length
Of destiny's cruel desire
Throw off your chains
We know their names'

When she finished singing, there was nothing but silence around us. Her singing voice was beautiful and there was so much emotion in the music. I didn't need to ask if that one of her father's songs; the tears streaming down her face answered that. Wiping away her sadness she strode over to the blade and it sang as it was plucked from the dirt.

"Let's do it," she said with a gritty smile, and then pushed past the cheering crowd back towards the gate.

Avar was waiting for us back near the old woman's hut. "Sorry Brin. I shouldn't—"

"Forget it, Avar. Just let it go," she barked at him.

Avar nodded and turned away with the shame still lingering in his eyes. "I think I can get us in. Follow me."

Follow we did. He led us near the gate and motioned for us to stay. The line at the gate had thinned, and one half of gate doors was closed. It was down to one guard at the entrance and only a few on the walls. Seeing the poster on the wall, I pulled my tattered hood over my head, trying to hide my face. Through one of the holes I could see Avar just casually walk up to the guard and start talking. Right away he had the guard laughing and it was like the two of them were old friends. The clouds overhead parted a bit to reveal the silvery moon hanging over us. Avar took a big long look up at the moon and smiled. He pointed at it and the guard's gaze

Chapter 7

followed. A few more words from Avar was all it took and they were shaking hands. Both he and the guard waved us over and we quickly passed through the gate.

"Remember, the berries," Avar told the gaurd. "Your wife will love it."

The guard laughed, "You have a good night, sir."

Once we were out of earshot and back in the narrow streets of Yellow Liver, Brin could not help but ask, "What did you say to that guy?"

"Just gave him some friendly advice. Kindness can go a long way," he said with a knowing smile. Whatever else he had done, he certainly wasn't going to explain it.

"Uh huh. Well, the barracks where the captain stays is over this way, I think."

"After you, m'lady."

Brin just rolled her eyes and started leading the way.

Sneaking through dark side streets with the narrow buildings looming over us we stalked to our destination. Every major street had posters with my face on them, so we tried to avoid areas with people. It wasn't hard, as most people had retreated to the safety of their homes or into a pub to wash away their day. Occasionally we would have to hide in an alley to let a patrol go past.

"It feels like we are going in circles," I whispered.

"We are, kinda. Weaving through the back streets, it is harder to tell where we are. If you would like to have a go at leading, Mr Posterface, you are more than welcome."

"No, it's ok. I don't know the city at all. I'm just worried that's all." My thoughts kept drifting back to the Ghoul who attacked me in the street.

"Isn't whining usually Avar's job?"

"Yeah! Stop stealing my thing, Spicy."

Annoyed with the nickname I said, "Somehow I don't think my name means Spice Rack."

"Well, what kind of rack is it then?"

Changing the subject, I asked, "Why is my face on those posters anyway?"

"My guess is that one of our friends survived your rescue."

Something inside told me that she was incorrect. There was a deeper, darker meaning that I just couldn't yet see. It worried me. It started lightly raining, which made our passage easier, but once we were all soaked, Avar started shivering. Through the rain and stink of the city, Brin pressed on, determined as ever.

"There, I think I see the barracks."

Short and wide, the barracks sat in an open court. The stone of the court was divided into sections for different kinds of training and marching. There were lights coming from nearly every window in the building, but we only saw figures moving on the top floor. Hesitating in an alley nearby, we all paused to think about what the next step was.

"Maybe I can just walk up and ask to speak to the captain."

"Separating is a bad idea, Avar. We don't want our celebrity getting attacked by magically appearing ghouls or anything."

"All the buildings here have cellar access from the street. Maybe we can use that, if it has one."

"Ok. Lemme scout it."

"What happened to sticking together?" His words went unheard by Brin as she crept across the court.

My eyes kept looking at the tops of the buildings around us. Out of the corner of my eyes, I kept thinking I saw movement. The longer we sat there, the more anxious I became. Avar's entire focus was on the court ahead and watching Brin. She disappeared

Chapter 7

around the corner of the barracks, and Avar became very fidgety. Time seemed to almost stop as we waited there for some sign from her. At one point I thought I heard something above me on the roof of one of the buildings next to us.

"You hear that?" I asked.

"Hear what? All I hear is the rain."

"I think there is something—"

"There she is!" Avar interrupted. "She's waving for us to come. C'mon, Wrack!"

The rain fell harder than I had ever seen it, and we scampered through the quickly forming puddles across the courtyard. Once behind the building, we saw the cellar doors and the half windows that revealed the cellar itself. While Brin and Avar worked on the lock, I peered in. It looked like most of the cellar was an armory. Swords, armor, livery bearing the black and red standard of the guard, bows, and shields were all stocked in a very organized holding room. Dressing tables lay about, too. Seemed like it was big enough for at least twenty men to get ready for battle simultaneously, but with more arms than three times that number. One corner of the room was separated from the rest by movable walls. Inside there was a special bunk room which seemed to be more decorated than I would have expected. Banners, flags, maps, books, and scrolls decorated the shelving and stands around the room. A very small bed and a fairly large desk were the rest of the furnishings. There was also a grey haired man sitting in the candlelight pouring over the maps on his desk. He seemed to be talking to someone in his room that I could not see, and the rain made it impossible for me to hear what he was saying.

"Got it! We have to move quickly because of the rain. You boys ready?" Brin asked.

Wracked

We both nodded, and Brin opened the cellar door just slightly to let us sneak in. We made enough noise that I was surprised to see that there was no one rushing down into the armory to investigate. As quietly as we could with drenched clothes, we sneaked through the dressing tables and arms to get to the curtained-off doorway of the captain's room. We could hear his voice, but couldn't make out anything until we got right next to the doorway.

"I have checked and checked with him, and he has no expectation. He is more consumed with looking for this death-touched man than with anything that goes on outside the city."

There was a hissing sound that seemed like a chorus of snakes that responded to the captain.

"Yes. We are all ready. When should we expect forces to arrive?"

More hissing sounds mixed with some quiet gurgling responded to his question.

"What the uzk is he talking to?" Brin whispered.

"I dunno."

Avar was not satisfied just to hear what was going on so he pulled back the curtain a bit to look. Moving an inch at a time, he kept pulling at the curtain trying to get a better angle into the room. Light from the captain's room filled his face and I saw the moment that his curiosity changed to surprise. Eyes wide, his head quickly turned to look and Brin and me and then back into the room.

"What?" Brin whispered.

He turned and looked at us again and, forgetting he was holding onto the curtain, he started to try and explain what he saw. This had one unfortunate consequence, as the curtain came falling down, pulling the wooden rod with it. It fell to the floor with a dull clunk and left Avar crouching in the doorway stunned.

Chapter 7

"Go block the door from upstairs," Brin commanded me as she drew Ukumog. *Clink*!

I ran across the room and started shoving one of the heavy dressing tables up against the stairway door. The grinding the wooden feet made on the stone floor did not mask the sounds of combat and muffled exclamations that were coming from the captain's room. The table got stuck on a stone not far from the door, and I heard heavy footfalls starting to trample the floor above me. Swiftly, I ran around the table and pulled it over the obstacle, straining to pull it closer to the door. Feet on the stairs on the other side caused my muscles to come alive with a wave of electricity. Heaving the table to chest height, I slammed it in front of the door, just as I heard feet come to the bottom of the stairs. Feeling sure that the door was blocked, I ran back into the captain's room. There was a splash and a loud crash just as I came into the room.

The grey haired captain was in the corner behind the desk, fighting off both Avar and Brin with a sword and shield. Avar kept getting in Brin's way. On the floor in front of the desk was a grey stone bowl partially filled with water and a dark splash of the same water on the stone floor near it. I quickly assumed that the bowl had been knocked off the desk, but felt that it was important and rushed over in that direction.

Papers were tossed all over the room as Avar climbed on the captain's desk so that he and Brin could both get at him. Being no newcomer to combat, the captain used his shield to swipe Avar's ankles, and Avar slipped and fell on the desk, hitting his head hard, but not before his mace came down to strike the captain in the face. Brin used this moment to surge forward and attack. Ukumog clashed with the captain's sword, and he growled first with his own voice followed by an unearthly echo of that growl. Distracted by that unusual sound, I stopped in my tracks. I looked down at Avar. His eyes had rolled back into his head.

"Avar? Avar?!" He still seemed to be breathing.

The captain saw me across the desk, and his focus changed. With strangely inhuman strength, he used his shield to push Brin back. She stumbled back onto the little bed that lay in the other corner of the room. My eyes met with the captain's for the first time. A feral fury lived there. Two things happened in that moment. The one I noticed was that some of the skin on the captain's face wriggled a tiny bit then tore free, revealing a rotting skull underneath. The mask of torn flesh waved around the back of his head like a mass of floating seaweed caught in a waving current. Startled by this horrifying display, I stepped back into the spilled water.

"Holy uzk! What the uzk are you?" came from Brin's corner as she leapt back to her feet.

The captain just hissed and gurgled in her direction mockingly. Disgust became hatred on her face, and she drew her other sword and charged forward at the captain with a storm of silver and black steel.

The other thing that happened in that moment when our eyes met, I did not see until it was too late. I felt something strong and sinuous wrap itself around my ankles. When I looked down, I saw that the dark water had recollected into a strange dark tentacle made of several branching lines. The skin of the slightly translucent body was a mass of shapes and forms. I thought I could see bits of faces, eyes, teeth, and hands all trying to push their way through the surface of it. Just under its skin, a thick dark fluid pulsed back and forth. Firmly rooted in the bowl, it continued to wrap itself around my legs until it got just past my knees. The free end of it

Chapter 7

rose to within inches of my face, the many strands opening like a hand with seven fingers, and within I saw a single bloodshot eye and a mouth full of razor sharp teeth.

The clashing dance of swords continued on the other side of the desk, with Brin bringing a seemingly endless assault of blades. The Captain seemed unfazed behind his battered shield, and as Brin kicked him trying to break his knee, he gracefully stepped to the side and sliced open her leg. Ukumog came down on the captain's shield with angry retribution, finally breaking it in two and showering the room with splinters. Fragments of wood flew into the mass in front of me and stuck like shrapnel landing in a jar of jelly, but the creature did not even react. The bloodshot eye looked over my face with malice and I could see it trying to decide what to do. Refusing to be helpless, I acted.

Lunging forward I wrapped my hands around the slippery mass just below the face of the thing. It was clearly stronger than me, as it tossed me back and forth. The coil around my legs tightened and I felt my joints pop and my ankles shatter. Screaming, I became more determined to hold onto this hissing, gurgling thing. It snapped its teeth at me and let loose an ear piercing howl. The pain in my legs forced a yell from me as well, quickly changing from a weak cry of pain to a howl of anger. Fear entered the bloodshot eye and the fingers at the end of the tentacle started waving around at me, trying to grasp at my hood or face.

The captain continued to defend himself from Brin with only the one blade and half the shield. He leapt up onto the table in one nimble jump, knocking Avar to the ground on my side of the desk. Continuing his strategic retreat, he charged out the doorway into the armory. Chasing him, Brin swung her legs around and slid across the desk, bringing Ukumog down just in time to have it rip into the captain's back.

123

Wracked

Breathing. The sounds of my own breath was all I could hear. Under my feet was a wet grassy soil. The smell of spilled blood and sweat filled my nose. The horizon of my vision took in the aftermath of a battle. Hundreds of bodies in various forms of burns, dismemberment, and disintegration lay strewn around me. A great circle of death surrounded me. The sky hung peacefully over me in the way that only the sky after a battle can look. From my hands drifted a tiny wisp of black and purple steam. Turning to my side, I suddenly noticed someone standing next to me. Half covered in blood, he greeted my glance with a warm smile. His green eyes were welcoming and charming.

"Kcarw, thgirla uoy?"

Confused, I watched him as the wind seemed to be blowing his hair backwards. A great anxiety grew inside me like the sound of avalanche going in reverse. I heard the sound of a chime and everything was filled with a cold darkness. I stood with my arms raised and the chaotic swirling black was surging into me as if I were calling it home. Vile screams of death and the sounds of hundreds of bodies being torn asunder played backwards in my ears. Comforted and confused, I continued to absorb the violent surge of purple and black until it was gone and I was surrounded. Hundreds of dried faces stared at me. I felt something at my back, and it was the charming green eyed man.

"I'll show you my power." I said with growing hatred.

"Where is your power now?" said the laugh's deep gravelly voice.

Chapter 7

Slowly the hundreds of hollow yellow faces crept maliciously backwards. In this ocean of dried, undead things I heard a hateful laugh. It was the same laugh of the pointy bearded commander. It floated over the ocean of undead soldiers, mocking me. My fear became hatred and I was now in control of it.

Like breaking the surface after nearly drowning, I gasped for air, my hands still locked around the tentacle creature in the captain's office. Looking around, I didn't see Brin or the captain, but heard the sounds of fighting from the armory. The piercing gaze of the bloodshot eye was looking unblinking at me. The anger I felt at my own helplessness grew in my chest. A biting cold entered my hands and I saw wispy streams of purple and black rising from them. Coils around me flexed again and the creature writhed violently. The coils loosened and I could feel it pulling away, trying to slip back into the bowl at its root. Anger and bloodlust drove me. The coldness surged and tore at the nerves in my hands as my hands became engulfed in purple flames.

"GRAAAAAAAAAAAA!" I screamed as I pulled my hands in different directions. The creature pulled and pulled, trying to pull even me into the bowl, but my size prevented it. A cacophony of popping and tearing, and I found the head of the creature in one hand and the trunk of it in another. One final high pitched unearthly wail was set free at the creature's demise and then it fell limp in my hands. Shocked at what I just did, I did not notice the flames disappear from my hands. The corpse melted in my hands and soon it was just a pool of dark ink laying on the stone. Stomping on the bowl, I cracked it and crushed it until it would never hold fluid ever again.

Wracked

Quickly, I rushed to the open doorway just in time to see Ukumog score a giant wound across the torso of the rotting captain. Immediately the room was filled with the horrible stench of rotting flesh and the captain fell lifeless to the ground. The runes on Ukumog were glowing brighter than ever before as Brin placed it gently back on her hip. *Clink!*

Our eyes met and we gave each other a smile before the sounds of the guards trying to break down the door brought us back to our situation. Grabbing Avar and his mace, we ran to the cellar door, and dragged him out into the rain. Just as my head cleared the diagonal threshold of the cellar, I saw a form hunched in the rain.

Lightning filled the sky with light long enough for both of us to get a good look at each other. Its dead eyes and grey skin told me that it was one of the city's ghouls. From where it was perched, it had seen everything that went on in the captain's room. I wondered how long it had been watching us. My gut told me that this was what I felt following us. Brin saw him too, and we both hovered in the open door with the rain pounding on us until we all heard the smash of the door crashing behind us. The noise startled our grey skinned onlooker too. He leapt to the roof of the building and crawled out of sight.

Voices behind us in the building pressed us to disappear into the wet narrow streets of the city. Lifting Avar onto my shoulders, we scampered through the falling sky to try and find refuge in this city filled with secret horrors.

Chapter 8

"We should find someplace full of people to rest and lie low."

I just nodded in a agreement with her. I followed her lead, trusting she knew where to go. The twisting narrow streets became tighter and tighter as we made our way deeper into the run-down portion of town. The southern and eastern parts of the town where we had spent all of our time looked rich in comparison to the north end. The people reflected the condition of the neglected and broken buildings that lurked over us. Many of the people seemed to have it worse than the people living in hovels outside the south wall. I wondered if these people also were robbed of their children in the night.

"Here we are. Gunna be horrid, but it should be safe." She opened the door to a large dark building that looked like a warehouse. Inside, there was a cloud of sick and weathered people. All of the eyes that I looked into seemed more like the eyes of a beaten animal than a person's. Coughing and shuffling were the only sounds that were in the building before we arrived, and it reeked of unclean life. Stopping in the doorway, I waited for Brin to scout us a place to hide. Some of the more curious and bolder of the people inside looked at us. Their stares were filled with a hunger. Some were hungry for food and others filled with other appetites.

Wracked

One young man looked at me with a hungry stare. My glare must have worried him, because he looked away quickly. Still, I knew his dark turn of mind. Brin pointed at a spot and we set ourselves there.

The place along the wall where we ended up was by no means secluded and Avar was still out cold. The wound to his head was not good. Once we got settled in a little, Brin used her skills on him and wrapped his head with more torn cloth. "I am going to need a new shirt after this." She laughed to herself.

"I think someone recognized me here."

"Oh yeah? Where is he? I'll make sure he keeps quiet."

"I don't see him anymore."

She gave a frustrated sigh. "I hope that doesn't come back to bite us."

We both watched over Avar silently for a few hours. Each moment that passed without the door being kicked in by someone looking for us made me slightly less tense. Brin, too, seemed to let the worry of our pursuers fade from her worries and she began slipping in and out of consciousness. "Go to sleep. I can keep lookout."

She nodded and lay down with her arms around the blade. "Sorry I didn't believe you about the ghoul before."

I just smiled and quietly sat nearby as she drifted off to sleep. The quiet hours that followed found me watching our company. Most of them just lay silently. Every short while, a few coughs would come from everywhere. People would shuffle around when water from the rains leaked in through a new spot on the roof, or the floor. Even more infrequently, someone would come through the large door and try and find somewhere dry to sleep. As the few candles in the place burned to their end or were blown out, I felt alone in the quiet dark.

Chapter 8

My eyes twisted into dark sight and I continued to scan my surroundings. People I had not noticed before were up in the rafters of the place where they had nested like birds. Every nook and cranny of this place was filled with quiet, desperate life. In my mind I was thinking about the power that surfaced in the captain's office. There in the dark where only I could see, I stared at my hands and tried to recall the cold dark flames that had been their gloves before. Hours drifted by while I was consumed by the desire to awaken whatever thing lay dormant within me, and only in rare moments could I bring a small tingle of the cold.

Growing frustrated, I stopped and started playing with some of the dirt on the floor in front of me. First I drew designs in the dirt. I started with things floating around in my head that didn't have any particular meaning. My mind wandered as I etched random lines into the dirt, erased them, and started over. A restlessness was growing inside me. Sitting there in the darkness, I was filled with a desire to take action. Too long had I been laying still; I felt it was time for me to act. The insecurity of my abilities kept bringing me back. *What would I do on my own? I can barely even defend myself.*

After mindlessly drawing in the dirt, it struck me what I had drawn. It was the black sun with eight rays waving away from it. Stunned and confused, I erased it. Then I looked over at the blade in Brin's arms. I drew each of the symbols on it that I could see, one at a time. I thought about each of them. It seemed as if I had seen them before, but no matter how much I mused on them, I could not decipher their meaning. There was something to them, though it was something that I could not see.

Avar stirred in his sleep, which told me that he was feeling a little better. Soon, light began poking holes in the building around us. Morning had arrived, and the people in the warehouse began to stir. Pulling my hood over my face, I just sat back into the shadow

Wracked

of our spot and tried to hide in plain sight. Soon thereafter, Brin awoke and started getting ready. Her face was still bruised from our last trip to Yellow Liver. The sheer force of will that kept her battered body moving was impressive.

"I am going to go out and see if there is any news and find us some food. Keep an eye on him, would you?"

"Yeah. Prolly best if I stay here."

Gently she smiled, then Ukumog greeted everyone in the room with a *clink!* Laying her bedroll over Avar to keep him extra warm, she waved at me and then headed out the door with the number of residents that were leaving. Only the sick and old were left behind. I wondered if they were permanent residents of this place, but this thought was disturbed when some people came back with a sack and put two or three of the people into them. Death, it seemed, was the unseen occupant of this place. I watched as the men carried out the bodies. There was no sorrow for those that had died and no signs that anyone here had even known them. Life in this place was emptier than I had first been led to believe.

Children outside the wall had families. Their loved ones wailed at their loss. These lost souls once had people like that. What path had they taken that led them to die alone in this nest of human rats? Poverty and oppression escaped in each cough. Turning inward I found myself struggling with my own thoughts.

"Obviously they deserve this fate. They are weak and the world is better off without them," stated one half of my mind.

"Every life has meaning because every life touches another. To remove those who are weak now weakens the lives that they touch, which leads to a cycle of destruction and death," replied the other.

Chapter 8

"So be it. At the end of the storm, only those who deserve their place will remain and on that iron foundation shall the world be rebuilt."

"Who are you?"

Malice and hatred filled my heart. My limbs grew cold. Opening my eyes, I saw the black steam leaving my hands. Shocked and scared I clenched my fists to make them stop. As I calmed, the steam faded.

"Where are we?" Avar said weakly.

"Avar? Don't move too much, you have a nasty wound on your head."

"Ugh. My head feels like it has been beaten in."

"It nearly was. Brin went off to get us some food."

"I had the weirdest dream. Alone and naked, I was stuck somewhere cold. Around me was nothing but darkness, but I lay in a pool of light, the column of which was so bright I couldn't look directly into it. Fighting the cold I stood up and looked around me. I was scared to leave the light, but after calling out to see if anyone was there, I thought I saw movement. Shielding my eyes from the light with one hand, I led with the other in front of me. Just as I broke the threshold of my protection, I saw them, hundreds of eyes unblinking in the empty space around me. I called out again, and just as I did I was attacked. Recoiling into the light, I saw that the arm I led with had gaping horrible wounds. I cried and reached to the source of the light and felt the disease in my blood being transformed. Standing up, I felt invincible. Just before I charged out of the light to combat my attackers, I woke up. Weird, huh?"

I found some comfort in the idea that I was not alone in having strange visions. Then I asked, "Do you think it means anything?"

Wracked

"Oh, I don't think I am blessed with prophetic dreams or anything. I just take it as a sign that the Lady is watching over me."

"Who is this Lady you are always going on about?"

"One of the gods. Though, people aren't allow to worship them anymore, they are still out there and people still do it, even if the punishment is death."

"I thought the gods abandoned the world after the Cursing."

"Some of them did. I only know that the Silver Lady still watches us from her place in the moon. The silver light can pierce even the darkest night, and so as long as we are open to her she will never be gone."

"I see. What about the other gods?"

He sighed. "Well, it is a little complex and there are millions of stories and old texts and things. To put it simply, there was a court of Gods headed by the King and Queen of the court. They had children and those children were the lords and ladies of the court. Half the court could be said to be immoral and represent the darker nature of man, the other side represent the illuminated courageous side, but the King and Queen sat neutrally above them all."

"And the Silver Lady is from the latter, right?"

"Yeah. She is the patron of artists, innocents, lore, purity. Throughout known history, she has played a subtle but powerful role in the events that unfolded."

"Interesting. Why is it that the Doomed have outlawed worship?"

"Because they fear it. Worship gives hope and hope leads to rebellion. Besides, they have become monsters that draw their power from outside the natural order of things."

"So magic came from the gods? I see."

Chapter 8

"Everything is tied together, my friend. Everything is tied together," he said with a big smile.

The conversation had a long enough pause that he fell back asleep. With so much to think about, I just let my mind churn at everything that was going on in my life. I assumed that it would resolve what it could and alerts would bubble to the surface if something needed my active attention.

Hours flew by, even in the stillness of the warehouse. Soon, Brin returned with food. She even brought some for me which I politely set to the side.

"What is going on out there?" I asked, politely.

"Well, there are still posters up everywhere, and there is news that the captain of the guard was killed last night by agents of the King."

"Well then."

"Yeah. I figure we can stay here for a few days then sneak out and maybe head up to Skullspill."

"Avar woke up, but I didn't ask him about last night. I figured you would want to be here for that."

She nodded and continued eating. We sat in silence for a while before Avar woke up and started eating his food.

"Wrack and I have talked about it, and after you feel better we are going to head to Skullspill." Brin informed Avar.

Surprised he responded, "We can't leave yet. There is an army on the way."

"Avar, there are only three of us."

"I don't care. That thing in the captain's office said that the Rotting One was only a day or so away. We won't have time to escape."

Wracked

"Uzk. And with the captain dead there is more paranoia and confusion in the streets. How are we supposed to fight one of the Doomed?"

"I dunno. I expect that the Ghoul might want to fight him off. They do work for different factions."

"Wait," I interrupted them. "The Rotting One and the Ghoul are both Doomed?"

"I explained this before, Spicy. The Rotting One works for The King, and The Ghoul works for The Baron."

His answer confused me even more, "And The Baron and The King are two of the powerful Doomed? The King is different than The King of the court, yeah?"

"Oh, they are different. Though The Doomed King thinks he is a god, just like the Baron does. They even have people that worship them and stuff. Which isn't outlawed."

Brin was tired of the history lesson, "Well, if you are already feeling better, maybe we should make plans to get the uzk out of here."

"Ugh. I am not ready to move just yet. Let's wait until tomorrow."

With that, the conversation ended. Brin was quietly fuming and went to sleep early. Avar's condition let him get even more rest. Night came quickly and so did the return of the desperate people of the warehouse. An old woman with nearly lifeless eyes found her way next to me and the room filled up more than it had the night before. In the deep dark of night, I again turned my thoughts to the strange power that lived in me.

Playing with the dirt again, I found myself drawing out of boredom. Again I drew the black sun. Curiosity drove me to do something strange and I bit my finger until it bled. Droplets of my viscous black blood fell into the middle of the circle. Mixing it

Chapter 8

with the dirt my mind became a torrent of dark thoughts. So many at once that I was unable to focus on anything more than the brief glimmer of images flooding my mind. A pain in my head started to grow and I felt the coldness enter my hands. The sensation of the steam rising from my hands began, yet I could not see the black streams floating upward. The dark blood in the circle of the sun started moving and shaping itself. Eyes wide, I stared at the strange thing that was unfolding before me. It sprouted malformed arms and legs into a vaguely humanoid shape. A head with a small misshapen face appeared on the tiny form. Its whole body was only slightly bigger than my thumb. The desire to name this thing grew in me until I could not hold it back, and a name sprouted forth from my lips—"Murks"—and gave life to the tiny thing.

It stretched and yawned as if it were waking from a long nap.

"Uzk, you are a hemodan, aren't you?"

"Yes master. Murks is glad to return to his master." It stood and came over to my hand where it grabbed one of my fingers and shook it like you would a friend's hand.

"Return to me?"

"Oh yes master. Murks has been asleep for a long time. Glad to be awake again."

I was both excited about this new little friend and worried what Avar and Brin would say about it. "Murks, these are my friends, but they can't know you are here."

"Ok, master. Murks will hide in his special place until you need him." With that, Murks climbed up on my robe and hid in a little pocket near my heart that I hadn't even noticed before. It was almost like it had been made just for him. "Master's robe is in disrepair. We should see if we can fix it later."

Wracked

"We will worry about that later, Murks." My curiosity spent, I sat back against the wall and tried to make the racing thoughts in my head die. There was something new there. A channel of my mind was open and I could sense the pocket within my robe. *What have I just done?*

Mind wheeling in no discernible direction, I lost track of time and my surroundings for a while. A creaking brought me back to the warehouse. Scanning the darkness, I saw only more rag clad visitors to the open room. Something was different, though. Hair on my arms started to stand and I became hyper aware of everything around me. It was not fear that inspired this sudden change of excitement. The cool electricity of a predator was my demeanor; this realization is what brought concern and fear.

The small group of newcomers were met by someone who was already here, and with them came a looming presence that I could not define. At first I thought it was just my own sense of dread, but I could not quash it. Forcing my eyes to twist through the black room I recognized the man who met them. He was the same one who stared at me when we first arrived. My instincts told me that there would be trouble, but decided to ignore them for the moment. Hood over my head, I tried to blend in with the pool of shadow in which I sat.

He talked to the six or seven newcomers. My ears reached through snoring, wheezing, and coughing to catch the words he was uttering.

"...Please don't think that, m'lord. He is here, I swear it. I am but a feeble man, and I cannot pierce the darkness as you can."

There was a gurgling chuckle that came from some of the newcomers. Stretching the power of my vision I examined them, looking for some sign that they were just human. Silently I cursed

Chapter 8

the fact that my dark sight drained most color, as I could not tell if the exposed skin was grey like that of the ghoul that had attacked me.

"Doubtless you would not lie to me. If you have, doubtless I will eat your children's hearts and make you watch as their blood empowers me." The tattered newcomer's voice sent a shiver down my spine.

"Please m'lord. I am your humble servant. If you find him to be here, please return my children to me." He started to fall to his knees, and the clawed hand of his conversational partner lifted him back to his feet.

"Doubtless your begging and scraping will alert him, fool. Remain here as I seek him out."

With glowing eyes, the disguised ghoul slowly started looking over the sleeping crowd. His friends surrounding the man and quietly watched him with hungry eyes. Frozen for a moment, I was unsure what to do. Running to the door would alert them, and would not lead to escape. The windows in the building were all within the area of the rafters. There seemed to be no way out.

The ghoul drifted through the rows of the desperate masses, each moment drawing ever closer to the shadow I occupied. Next to me Avar lay sleeping and on the other side of him was Brin and the blade. For a moment I thought that perhaps I could grab the blade and fend off this fiend. Like a bolt, my mind turned back to the fight with the horror in the captain's office. Closing my eyes, I tried to recall the cold power to my limbs. Footfalls and creaking floorboards distracted me. He was drawing ever closer. Panic started leaking into my mind. His claws flexing and relaxing as he pursued me. Eagerly his glowing eyes searched for mine. Amidst the rank of filthy people, the smell of death drifted to my nose and I could hear his teeth grinding as he stalked me.

Wracked

Flashes of cold came to my limbs and faded as quickly as they appeared. My body became restless, and I had to fight my own impulses to shift and move.

"Master? Should Murks do something?" Came a whisper in my head.

No Murks, stay still. I tried to return the thought and felt him relax in his hidden pocket.

Only a few rows away now was my hunter. Breathing heavily, I tried to calm the panic. With each step the struggle became harder. I knew it was only a matter of time before he saw me. The indecision to wake my friends wrestled in my heart as I tried to see every outcome. Only a row away, I saw his claws dancing with the black talon that had stabbed me. He rolled it through his sharp digits like a child mindlessly playing with their favorite toy.

"Avar," I whispered, quietly nudging him. "Avar. Avar, wake up."

Sleepily opening his eyes, he went to say something. Both eyes opened in shock when I placed my cold hand over his mouth. Subtly, I pointed to my stalker and Avar nodded. Turning as if in his sleep he faced Brin and started poking at her. The ghoul was twenty five paces away. Twenty four.

"Mmh. What?" Brin said in her usual morning discontent.

The ghoul stopped in its tracks one row away from me. Turning slowly he came to face me. His features were sullen and ferocious, chin stained permanently with the blood of innocent souls that had passed through the gate of death that sat hungrily above it, strands of greasy hair spilled out through the tattered rags around his head, nose sunken almost like that of a skull, and eyes wide and large glowing there in the darkness.

"Oh uzk." Brin had seen it and her exclamation caused it to look away from me for a moment.

Chapter 8

"Doubtless we have some guests. Send our friend to see his children." A disappointed ghoul in the back took the man out of the building, the rest of them surrounded their leader, maliciously stepping on sleeping, people as they went. Noise of people waking filled the house, noises which quickly became whispering and gasps. Sitting as still as possible I wished that I could just melt into the shadows and vanish.

"What? No grand speech or violent flair for us? Doubtless you have lost your edge," the leader of them spoke to us.

"How's this for an edge?!" Brin leapt from her sleeping place with Ukumog glowing brightly in her hands. Strange shadows were cast across the faces of the ghouls from the glowing sigils on the blade. The leader's face twisted into raw unmixed hatred and he stabbed the black talon into his own clawed thumb. My blood felt as if it were on fire.

"Aww. Doubtless your pain is delicious. You will fear my new power. Doubtless the shadows will send you back to the forgotten place from where you crawled." Near the ghoul, darkness swelled together, and with a bass popping sound appeared three skinless dogs which looked formed of completely charred flesh. Before their snarls could even be heard, a ripple of panicked people started fleeing from the horrors like a storm swirling around us. Standing in the eye of this storm of fear, the ghoul and his minions gave us a twisted smile. Ukumog's glowing runes became a blur of blueish light and the fight had begun.

Screams and commotion filled the entire building. Avar grabbed his mace and charged in to watch Brin's back. The agile ghouls made them work twice as hard to score any kind of hit. I stood up and the leader's hateful scowl focused on me and he reached his hand beneath his torn shirt. A brace of daggers came out from there with the claw. With a couple quick flicks, the sharp weapons pierced my shoulders. The force of the attack threw me back against the wall, impaling me to the wall slightly off the floor.

Skinless dogs tore at everything near them, which was mostly helpless people trying to escape the scene. Blood quickly flowed along the floor. Each of the ghouls had a euphoric expression on its face at the smell of the blood in the air, driving them into a frenzy. No longer were they focused on Brin and Avar, but every weak and tender person around them. Within seconds, the entire scene devolved into a gore drenched feast. Limbs and bodies flew in every direction, the ghouls themselves fighting over each savory bite of human flesh.

Scoffing in disgust at the actions of his minions, the leader of the ghouls retreated to the doorway. Before he slipped out the door, he looked at me menacingly and moved a claw across his throat. Cackling as he vanished, the door was pulled shut behind him.

Now trapped in the room with these hungry beasts of flesh and shadow, Brin and Avar went back into action, attacking the creatures as they tore and ripped at their prey. Pain shot through my body as I tried to pull the daggers out of my shoulders. After moving it around, and causing waves of crippling pain, I was able to free one dagger. With one shoulder free, I swung painfully from the other pinned shoulder.

Before I could do anything else, the dogs were at me. They chomped on my legs and started pulling at me like a wishbone. The sounds that came from me matched those screams that had originally been my waking pulse. Such pain I had not really experienced, and at first I found it debilitating. Suddenly, something inside me started to burn the pain as fuel. A pulse ran through me, filling me with electricity and strength. Wave after wave of vitality

Chapter 8

rocked through me. Heat started rising from my eyes, and my hands went numb with cold. Pulling against the strength of the dogs, I was simply able to keep them from tearing me apart, but as the waves came, I found myself dragging them back together.

With a sickening pop and thud, I fell from the wall. I pulled the dagger from my shoulder and watched my black blood drip from it once before springing to action. With a dagger in each hand I sat up and drove each dagger into the skull of my attackers. The blades were long enough that the tips just barely pierced the surface of the dog's skin under its jaw. Still surging with strength, they both kept tearing at me. I twisted and turned the daggers along with the heads that they had become impaled in. Bones cracked and tendons popped. Cold rushed from my hands into the weapons and I felt myself drinking the dark power of these creatures. Instantly my wounds closed and my mind filled with iron hate. My hands tore the daggers from their places with such force that ripped the dog's heads from their bodies, and with one fluid motion I found myself standing between their broken bodies.

Dancing in the darkness before me, I saw Ukumog in Brin's hands, the sigils glowing brighter than I had ever seen them. My heart beating with power and excitement, I hungered for more death. Hypnotized by the blade doing its work, I almost felt it ask me to join it there, a request I could not refuse.

I ran into the thick of the fray. Claws and teeth. Blade and mace. A cacophony of wet cutting, tearing, and smashing. The glory of my bloodlust erased all morality and questions from my mind. Here in this whirlwind of death, I felt at peace. In a few short moments, there were only a few of the ghouls left. Avar had bashed a few of them to death, and the deadly combination of Brin and Ukumog had severed at least an equal number limb from limb.

Wracked

The three of us forced the remaining few into a corner, where they fought like a pack of desperate animals. Before we could seal their fate, the roof of the warehouse crashed to the floor in the corner opposite in a hail of metal and flame. A handful of people were crushed under the wreckage and more still were trapped underneath. A few of the ghouls took this distraction as an opportunity to try and escape. Chased to the door, they found that the door had been locked from the outside just before Avar and I collided with them. One of them raked his claws across my face which healed so fast it was like water coming together after a child ran his fingers through it. I smiled as I drove my daggers into his surprised face with such force that I broke both blades against the back of his skull. Within a few moments, they were all dead.

Both Brin and Avar showed wounds from the fight. The only evidence that I had been involved was the black blood on my skin.

"Guess some of your past came back, eh?" Brin was impressed.

Avar was excited, "Wow, Wrack. That was amazing! Where did you learn how to fight like that?"

Not able to answer his questions, I found myself grinding my teeth.

"Wrack, Brin, help me try and free some of these people!" He said as he rushed over to the rubble.

The night sky above us was filled with smoke, and the warehouse was quickly catching fire. Many of the people within were wailing and crying, others had given up and were willing to accept their fate. The ones who hadn't given in to their despair put their nervous fear to work trying to help Avar free people. We had to find a way out.

Chapter 8

"This whole place is going to come down, Avar. We need to find a way out of here!"

He nodded and continued trying to free the living from the fallen roof. Brin and I looked around for some way out. Scanning the now brightly lit room, I could see no way out unless we could fly. "What about the hinges?"

"What?" She yelled through the growing noise inside.

"Chop at the wood around the hinges. If we can break the wood we can escape!"

"That is a lot of chopping, I don't think that is going to work!"

"You got a better idea? Or would you rather burn to death?"

"Fair enough!" She moved over to the big warehouse doors and paused for a moment looking at Ukumog. "Sorry, my other blade has no chance at busting us out." She said to the blade before raising it to clash with the old wood around the door.

Looking around, the fire was continuing to spread. I decided to kick at the door while she was cutting at the wood figuring that something had to give. The fire in the collapsed portion of the building had grown too great for any more people to be rescued, so Avar and all his helpers gathered around us at the door. Trying to drown out the howling cries of the trapped people burning to death, I kept kicking at the door. It seemed to be weakening.

"Everyone come here and bash this door with me. Brin, you keep chopping."

With the sixteen or so of us bashing on the door in unison while Brin cleaved at the wood, we seemed to be making progress. Cracks appeared, then got wider and wider. Soon there was a huge gap in the wall, but it was still not large enough for us to escape. That did not stop some of the desperate to try and force their way out, getting in Brin's way.

Wracked

"GET THE UZK OUT OF THE WAY!" She screamed at people who paid her little mind. They all seemed to mutter defensive things about their children who need them.

Do any of these people actually have children?

Brin's rage got the better of her and she started shoving and kicking people out of her way while Avar, myself, and a handful of people continued to work on the door. Inside the heat was becoming unbearable. Sweat was pouring off everyone's skin, making the rank odor of unwashed people even worse. The heat and her anger broke Brin's will and she let Ukumog loose on one of the people trying to climb out of the crack. His body fell lifeless to the ground and everyone got away from her. Like nothing had happened, she just went back to working on the wall.

The floorboards engulfed in flames, some of the people crowding the door started to catch fire. Panic hit everyone. I could feel the fire spreading behind me as people on fire tried to press their way into space that was not engulfed of which there was none that did not have people. Heat from the fire continued to press towards us.

"This is UZKIN' useless!" Shouted Brin.

Avar seemed almost ready to give up, "So this is it. By the Lady I didn't think it would end this way."

"It's not over yet." I said.

I saw the hope renewed in his eyes from my statement, and he smiled. As most of the roof had fallen away, the exposed night sky was filled with a mix of smoke, embers, and moonlight. A beam of light hit Avar's face and a calmness came over him. "One more time, shall we?"

Chapter 8

I nodded. Avar counted to three then we all kicked the door that was now on fire. With a booming crash the door and part of the fiery wall fell into the street on the outside. Like rats, people fled in every direction.

The streets outside were chaos. First I thought it was just us. Watching the streets around us, I was wrong. People fled in every direction. Looters broke into buildings. Guards ignored the chaos and ran to the city walls. The siege of the city had already begun.

"What the uzk is going on out here?" Brin asked.

Avar looked around for a moment, "I think the Rotting One is already here, Brin."

"Uzk."

"That one ghoul had strange powers. I wonder if he was THE Ghoul." Avar seemed almost happy about our encounter.

The possibility that I was being hunted by one of the Doomed hadn't crossed my mind until that moment. I recalled a vague recognition in the ghoul's eyes. If he was one of the Doomed, I was in a lot more trouble than I had originally thought.

"The Doomed are all very powerful right? Why would he come after us?"

"Dunno. But there was definitely something different about him." Avar told me.

Something huge and on fire whooshed over our heads and destroyed a nearby building making all three of us dive for cover.

Brin's pragmatic mind kicked in, "Uzk this. Let's get out of here."

We all agreed. Soon we were back to our usual behavior of Brin leading us through the streets. This was anything but normal, however. The streets were clogged with panic and greed, along with the shifting pathways due to collapsed buildings or fire. Turning a corner we found ourselves face to face with a small gang of people wearing mismatched bits of armor. Behind them was a group of women all tied together and sitting in a pile looking distraught. One of the men came forward and an evil grin appeared on his tattooed face.

"Well well well. What do we have here? How much you want for her, boys?"

Brin was not even playing his game. *Clink!* Free flying went the blade and it made short work of the tattooed man. Immediately the other men ran in to fight us. The mace at Avar's side was also loosed and he supported Brin. Once again, I found myself with no weapons or strange power at my command. Forced to stand by, I watched the captured women. Each death of their captors lit a small glimmer of hope in their eyes, that is, until they spied my pale face. Their fear angered me, and I withdrew inward to seek the origin of that feeling. *Why was I upset that they found me frightening? Didn't I also find my dead form hideous when I first saw it?* The sounds of battle that surrounded my pondering slowed and then ended.

"Wrack? You ok?"

"Yeah, I am fine Avar. We should set them free."

"Uzkin' slaver scum." Brin kicked one of the dead bodies at her feet and spit at him. "Miserable people that profit from destroying families and creating misery."

"Not everyone can be as nice as you." A sarcastic smile accompanied Avar's comment, making Brin crack a smile.

"I know, I am such the charmer." She laughed.

The women who thanked Brin and Avar for saving them ran off in separate directions. Only one of them even acknowledged that I was there, and there was nothing but fear in her eyes. Dwelling in this fear, it reminded me of the boy. I imagined him locked in

Chapter 8

some horrible box drenched in the horrible ichor of ghoul drool from the monsters which lingered over him. The boy was brave, but even Brin might crack under those conditions.

Slipping off the main street Brin had something on her mind. "I think we should get the uzk out of here and head to Skullspill. We can't help these people anyway."

"We can't just leave the city to be destroyed. Have you seen what you can do with that sword? The three of us could help repel the Rotting One!"

"To what end, Avar? Ghoul, Rotting One, either way they live under the sadistic thumb of some greater evil thing! We gotta worry about out own skin here."

"When are you going to accept that perhaps there are greater things afoot here than your father's death? It happened twenty five years ago! I doubt us trying to do a little good along the way will make the trail go cold."

"Uzk you, Avar. If you don't like what I am doing, you don't have to stay with me. You can run back to your moonlit sanctuary and pretend that the world can be fixed."

There was another crash nearby that froze whatever words Avar was about to speak. It was my voice that filled the silence. "Stay or go, doesn't matter to me. As long as we save the children that those things have taken. That, we can change."

Both my companions looked at me with blank faces. A smile appeared on Avar's face first, and the cold edge to Brin melted slightly.

"Save the children," she said and stopped to take in the chaos around us. "Ok. Let's do it. Probably stupid, but . . . Let's do it."

Wracked

All in agreement, we stepped back into the fiery madness of the war that surrounded us. Weaving through the insanity Brin shouted, "How do we find them?"

Avar pointed, and both of us turned to see a grey skinned ghoul sitting alone in an alleyway, devouring the dead remains of a solider. "He'll know."

"So, we make him tell us," I stated coldly.

Chapter 9

Bolting after the distracted ghoul, Brin was quick and efficient with her approach. Avar and I tried to keep up, but the fast moving panic that surrounded us prevented that. A guardsmen running through the crowd hit me with his shield accidentally and knocked me to the ground. By the time I got up, I saw that my friends were chasing our target towards the wall.

"Hey!" I shouted at no one in particular as I tried to catch up.

The ghoul was loping around on all fours most of the time, giving it an extra measure of dexterity and speed. As it approached the city wall, it bounded off the wall to a nearby building then onto the wall itself. To my shock and surprise, Brin was able to do the same thing with a few quick kicks of her legs, leaving Avar and me on the ground below. Shock, which fast became anger, filled the gluttonous face of the ghoul. It continued trying to escape by running down the length of the wall. This was no easy task, as the wall was scattered with guards dressed for battle. All of them let the ghoul pass with some surprise, but many of them tried to hinder Brin. The first of which she just shoved off the wall and the second she slashed open with Ukumog, then she leapt to the building near the wall and followed the ghoul by jumping from rooftop to rooftop, sending a shower of shingles down on Avar and me. We kept running trying to find someway to get into the chase ourselves. Finally a stone stairway that led to the top of the wall came to us.

Smoothly ascending the stairs, Avar grabbed a shield from a dead guard who was laying halfway on the steps. The action of removing the shield sent the body down into the street below, and Avar remained focused on the ghoul. There was a clatter of leather on stone and Brin had rejoined us. Avar, now in front, used the shield to push past the soldiers on the wall as we rapidly closed the gap on the slowing ghoul. It kept looking out at the dark expanse outside the wall. Following its glance I looked out beyond the city.

There was enough light that I could see a sea of movement. Silhouettes of men and siegeworks covered the open area outside the wall. The chatter and sounds of battle were a soup of noise, making it impossible to focus on any one thing. The light in the field came from many fires that had either been started by flaming arrows that were being shot from the walls, or by the great balls of fire that were being lobbed into the city by their fierce looking catapults. Ladders were being thrust up against the walls and more often then not they were repelled by the men defending the city. A massive ram lay dormant in the middle of a constantly shifting sea of arms. Every few moments, the men pushing it would be forced to defend themselves from oncoming volleys of arrows,or they would fall, only to be replaced seconds later by one of their compatriots. The shouting and screaming all seemed to happen in a controlled chaos. How any of this made sense was beyond me. I could not help but wonder why anyone would want this horrible city in the first place.

Distracted by the battle, I did not see when Avar stopped, causing me to run into him and slip and fall on the wet stone. Picking myself up, I saw Brin leap forward and dig the blade deep

Chapter 9

into the hind quarter of the ghoul. Watching this thing suffer filled me with a fire in my chest that I could not explain, but did not really question.

Screaming in pain, the thing let a few words fly, "No! Don't kill me! Let me go! So hungry!"

Ferociously, Brin seized the ghoul by the neck and lifted the blade up high enough so that it would be constantly reminded of its presence. Glowing ominously in the night, I was sure that the runes could be seen even by the soldiers down below. Guards on the wall who first moved to come to the ghoul's aid backed off as Avar and I stood guard on either side. Their eyes occasionally drifting to the thirsty edges of Ukumog. When they realized we were not there to attack them, they went back to their battle, but never ignored the fact that we were there.

"Tell me! Tell me where your master keeps the stolen people!"

"No stolen people! We eats them all." His face turned sadistic and hungry and he snapped his jaws at Brin.

Unflinching she tightened her grip and shook him making him choke. "Do not lie to me, you filthy puss bag. No doubt you sold your soul for this power that courses through your cursed body, but it will do you no good. This is Ukumog. You know its bite; just tell me what I want to know, or I might let it have its way with your flesh." Her biting calm hatred was unnerving, even to me.

Tears formed in the ghoul's milky dead eyes. His mouth quivered with fear and sadness. Brin's words had wounded the last shred of humanity left in this creature. "Sold my. . . So hungry. Master." It whimpered.

Brin shook him again. With her teeth clenched she brought the blade in closer. "I can end this torment for you. Tell me what I want to know and your haunted life will come to an end."

Wracked

Hope filled the creature's face. "We don't deserve your pity. We have done horrible things. Horrible. Horrible." Deep within the ghoul a rumbling noise roared. "So hungry. Can't stop. Master takes the most tender. The most delicious ones. Hides them in his sanctum. Deep in the heart of the under tunnels. The sewers. You find him there."

Brin loosed her grip a bit. The tension in her back relaxed slightly. "Does he have the place trapped?"

"Master is clever. Many tunnels lead to him, but only one can be used. Use the one that have the worst stink and you find him easy." Again the belly of the ghoul came to life, voicing its protest of its owners situation. "So hungry. So hungry!" Slowly, its arms were raised as if calling to the heavens for a release from its torment.

"How do we get in the sewers? Where is the nearest entrance?"

The hope in the ghoul's eyes faded. It looked at Brin with a coldness that was enhanced by those milky dead eyes. Brin drew in closer, gritting her teeth and tensing again. There was a moment of stillness between them that seemed to last forever. The battle that raged around us seemed to slow, but the violently fury of noise from it continued to flow through us.

"WHERE IS IT! TELL ME!" Screaming at him did no good. The hunger had taken over his mind. There was again a brief calm, then like lightning striking, his arms closed around Brin. The two of them struggled for a few extremely violent seconds, the ghoul tearing at her in a frenzy, and she trying to pry him off her enough to bring down the cleaving edge of Ukumog. Avar and I sprang into action. He brought his mace to bear down on the shoulder of the ghoul, and I grabbed Brin, trying to help separate

Chapter 9

them. The ghoul's face roared at me with a loud, wet, shaking wave of death odorous air. A claw tore into my arm, but I refused to let her go.

Pressed against her, I felt my body absorbing her warmth. A certain hunger for her heat came over me for a moment. I felt muscles in my body relax and the lids of my eyes became slightly heavy. My senses became keen to brilliant life that teemed within her and I knew a hunger all my own. Fighting with the ghoul and with myself, I continued to try and pull them apart. Almost drunk with the feeling of her warmth, I was not particularly effective at my task. In the tangled mess of this bloody fight, I felt Brin's sword arm move with a deadly purpose. Ukumog sang as it collided with the flesh and bone of the ghoul. I mentally braced myself for the oncoming horrible scream, but none came. Instead I hear an intense humming, and through the pile of limbs and torso that was the three of us I saw the burning blue runes of the blade.

In the void I felt empty. Floating in nothing I became aware of a weight slowly pouring into me. Bitter cold attacked me from inside and quickly the outside became cold. Opening my eyes I saw their faces. Men of power and ambition changing into something else. There was a sickness in their look, a growing coldness.

Something has gone wrong!

A narrow-faced man with slicked back black hair smirked at me. In his grey eyes I could see that he knew what was happening, that he had done this to us. In my mind I could see that the power was flowing through all of us, as if we were all connected by unseen black tendrils of writhing energy.

Wracked

A mind-shaking screech vibrated my thoughts and I was seeing two things at once. The men who were reveling in their waking power were now covered by a translucent curtain of another moment. The old bearded man who I had watched die over and over in my dreams was sitting in his chair in the tower. He was smiling and laughing while talking to me gently with words I could not understand. Stretched between two moments fear and sadness became my only emotions. A scream exploded from my lungs that terrified me. Tears painted my cheeks as the cold pushed most of the heat out of my body.

The gentle words of the old man filled me with a longing and emptiness. He touched my cheek and playfully poked my nose. A coin in his hand kept vanishing and appearing in funny places. Behind my ear was his favorite, each time he did it there was a glimmer of joy in his eyes. His laughter was echoed by the gleeful sounds of a young boy, a young boy that I knew was me.

Pain wracked my body, causing my limbs to surge out from me. My muscles became tight and felt as if they were going to tear themselves apart. Convulsing, I heard the greedy horrible laughter of my silk and armor wearing company. The marble floor met my body with an unforgiving crack as I crumpled to the floor and my head crash to the surface. Above me there was a domed ceiling. From within, my soul quietly cried out for help. My presence drifted away from me and upwards toward the grand mural on that ceiling. Drawn to its peaceful serenity, I was in awe of the circle of dragons which made up the intricate art above me. As I seemed to get closer to it, I embraced the colors and metals which were skillfully placed in each subtle detail of this ring of ancient titans, each of them displayed with their glories intact, each dragon holding the preceding one's tail in its mouth. At either end of the circle were dragons of many colors. One half contained images of a

Chapter 9

chromatic nature: red, black, blue, green, and white. After the other multi colored one were the metallic forms: gold, silver, bronze, brass, and copper. Closer and closer I got the more I seemed drawn to the silver dragon. Honing in, I stared at her face. There on the ceiling of the temple I saw in her eye a single tear. Unable to hold it back any longer, I succumbed to the numbing coldness of the pain that had invaded me and the color of the world was drained away. I felt death try and steal my warmth, but it was abated. Drawn away by something else, death let me remain, and it glided off to claim a different victim. The pain became part of me and I lay upon the floor, gasping for breath. There was no sound other than my quest for air for a long time.

"Is the ritual over then?" said a deep gravelly voice.

"Indeed brother. Do you not feel the power within you?"

"I do feel something. Yes. This is good. We will use this strength and this magical union to end the wars once and for all."

A rounding cheer from the crowd filled the smooth open temple only hindered slightly by the curtains hanging between each of the massive pillars holding the dome over our heads.

"That is if our invoker is not too much wracked with pain, eh?"

Hands from laughing men reached down to pull me up. There faced with them again, I saw the malevolent lust for power flickering behind all of their eyes. With a blink their faces were gone and I saw them as horrible dead things. Each of them changed in different ways, but before I could take in the details of their transformation I was returned to the shallow laughter of their false camaraderie. The gravelly voice I followed to the same pointed beard that was attached to the man in the macabre armor. The

Wracked

commander who slew the gentle old man of the tower. I choked back my hatred and my desire for revenge and laughed as falsely as the rest of them.

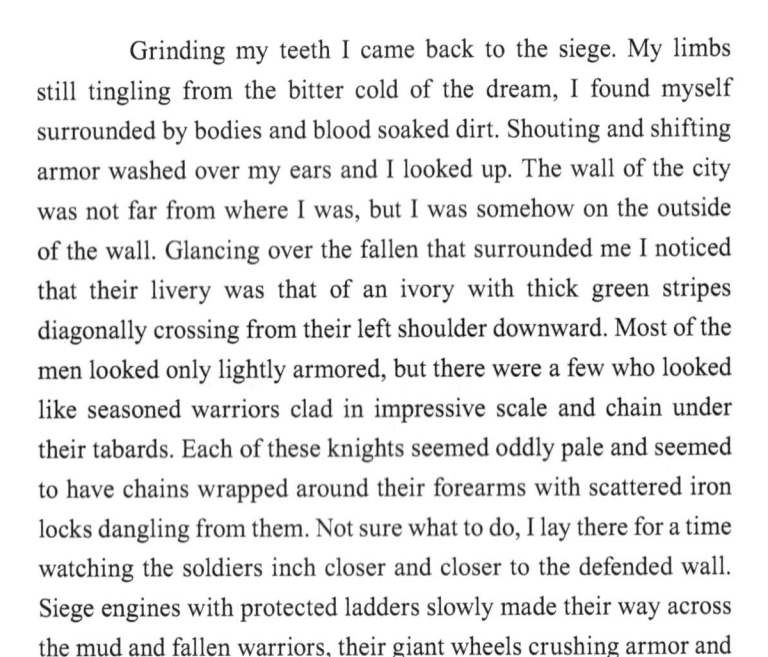

Grinding my teeth I came back to the siege. My limbs still tingling from the bitter cold of the dream, I found myself surrounded by bodies and blood soaked dirt. Shouting and shifting armor washed over my ears and I looked up. The wall of the city was not far from where I was, but I was somehow on the outside of the wall. Glancing over the fallen that surrounded me I noticed that their livery was that of an ivory with thick green stripes diagonally crossing from their left shoulder downward. Most of the men looked only lightly armored, but there were a few who looked like seasoned warriors clad in impressive scale and chain under their tabards. Each of these knights seemed oddly pale and seemed to have chains wrapped around their forearms with scattered iron locks dangling from them. Not sure what to do, I lay there for a time watching the soldiers inch closer and closer to the defended wall. Siege engines with protected ladders slowly made their way across the mud and fallen warriors, their giant wheels crushing armor and bones along the way.

"WRACK! WRACK!" Brin's voice came from somewhere above me.

"I'm down here!" I tried to respond through the messy clatter of the battle.

"WRACK! WRACK!" the voice cried from further away. She hadn't heard me.

Chapter 9

Alone again, it was as if it were the first time. Uncertain what to do, I stood there like the eye of the storm that raged around me. Men rushing towards their deaths all hoping to climb the ladders into the city. I went mostly unnoticed except for the occasional strange glance from someone mid battle shout, then I felt it, a strange presence that felt familiar yet unknown. There was a power here, outside the walls, that hung like the stink of something dead under the floorboards. Confusion arose from my internal conflict. *Should I try and find my way back in or seek it out?* Before I could make up my own mind, it was made up for me.

"You ain't one of us! HEY! He ain't one of us!" A grimy, hateful soldier stared at me calling to his friends around him. The small crowd of them turned towards me. "Who is you, dead thing? What master do you serve?"

Silently, I wished they would just ignore me.

"I'z talkin to you! Who is your master?"

"You mean, which of the Doomed? Which of the Doomed do I serve?" I asked.

"You ain't no servant of the Rotting one, and you don't look like you am a servant of the King. So who are ya?"

"Uh. I don't serve any of the Doomed. I was just—"

"You was just what?" They closed in on me, pleased that they had one of the enemy in their clutches. Their faces held echoes of the desire to cause pain that I had seen before on Larry the guardsman's face.

"I just fell off the wall, and now I am—"

"Oh, so you do serve one of the masters, then. You serve that wretched ghoul thing!"

"Oi, he doesn't look like wot I fink dem ghouls look like."

"Yeah, where hims fangs at?"

"They ain't got fangs you eejot. Dem have a giant maw fing."

"Himz ain't got no maw either."

The company behind the leader bantered while we two remained silent. He sized me up, and considering I wore nothing but tattered robes and had no weapon, I must have looked like easy prey.

"What we gunna do boys? Kill this one or take him back to the master?"

"I say we kills em."

"Oi, but bringin' him back alive might gets us rewarded."

"Ah. Good point. Leds bring him back den."

The desire to cause me pain had been replaced by greed in their eyes. I was certain that whatever master they served would be a worst host than them trying to kill me there in the middle of the fight.

"Right," The leader said. "We takes him back to the master. Question is, you comin' quiet-like or are we gunna have to rough you up a bit?"

Considering my odds of escape, it didn't look good for me. I figured that if I tried to escape, they would just cut me down and drag me back to their master like the dogs that they were. Stalling for time, I tried to call upon the power within me. I longed for the biting cold and black energy, but my thoughts still lingered on Brin's warmth. Frustrated, I battled with my body to purge this desire from me. I wanted to embrace the cold, bitter power. A trickle of fear entered my mind. *Will this lust for her warmth drive you to hurt her?* The mere idea of this event made my eyes swell.

"Aw. Look boys. He's cryin."

"Bah. The master will give him somethin' to cry about. Get him."

Chapter 9

Each plate of their armor scraped and clattered against the others surrounding it. The few that still had their weapons sheathed drew them, and I heard every inch of the metal grinding its way out of the scabbard. My eyes became slits and I saw them all charging me in slow motion. I felt like I had all the time in the world.

Elsewhere on the battlefield, I could sense a power drawing closer. I looked beyond the group of slow moving soldiers and couldn't find it amidst the intensely fueled, yet slow moving battle that quietly boiled all around me. There was a peace in that moment. Each piece of dirt and shouting face had a grace and beauty. The pure, ignorant hatred of the soldiers who did not care to know their enemy save that they were just that. Their pitiful lives so filled with oppression that they lashed out in any malicious way they could, just to bring some control into their lives. It all made sense, not something I was used to feeling. My life until that moment had been such a mystery. These people don't know any better. *What lives they must have where being this way seems fair, just, or right? Who would seek to make a world filled with such ignorance and fear?*

The swords of my attackers drew closer and so my pondering drew to a close. A still-biting pain wracked my spine. I felt charged with the power, and it was at my beck and call.

"Welcome back, master" Murk's voice was in my head.

Not sure how to respond, I didn't. I just commanded the cold pain to protect me and it obeyed. The speed of undeath faded and returned to that of the living. Black and purple smoke rose from my hands and with a FOOM I was surrounded by a bubble of translucent power. The eruption of this smoky shield collided with my group of attackers and threw them like ragdolls in all directions. All of the soldiers who could see me through the dark battle torn field paused for a moment and I let the shield fade. My lungs burned

Wracked

as I realized I hadn't been breathing and I felt as if my chest were going to explode. Gasping for air, I let the protective barrier fade and felt the cold painful power leave me.

"I am just me, Murks. Whatever you expect me to be, I don't think I am him anymore."

I felt that he acknowledged my response and was unsure about it. Picking myself up from the dirt, I looked toward the place where I felt the presence. Thinking about Brin and Avar climbing through the sewers to save the children without me was not something I wanted to happen. My curiosity would have to wait.

Moving to the wall, the soldiers on the field gave me a wide berth. Some even stopped fighting or working to whisper something unheard to themselves or their companions. The tide of the battle was surging towards one part of the wall. As I came closer, I saw that there was a huge hole in the wall. The battle had broken the levy and was now spilling into the city within.

Pushing my way through the men fighting wasn't hard. A few of them stabbed me with their swords or slashed at me as I passed. I accepted these temporary wounds as a toll for my crossing, and did not even look back to see the faces of those who dealt them to me.

Before I could get through the hole in the wall, the hair on my neck stood up. Powerful eyes were upon me. Instead of going through the hole into the city, I climbed the jagged wall and from about half its height looked out into the battle searching for the source of these eyes.

"So, it begins again," a man's laboring voice rasped into my thoughts.

I felt the world shake slightly as if the heavy footsteps of a giant were moving the very earth under my feet. All around me the battle continued in a muted silence. The lives of the people all

Chapter 9

around me seemed unimportant and almost like children playing. A form moved up to the horizon. Backlit by the fires of the catapults, a man stood there. From his silhouette, I gleaned his confidence and important bearing. He seemed to me an almost regal figure who heroically stood with his men in the midst of this battle.

"Begins? What begins?" I asked.

"Let us not play games, Wrack."

Pushing my eyes to the limit, I twisted in and out of my dark sight to try and pierce the darkness. As a man came running by with a torch the face of the man was illuminated. His salt and pepper hair bristled out like an unkempt bush, half his face covered by a tattered rag which held the fading detail of something which may at one time been beautiful. The other half of his face was not dissimilar. The frame of it was that of a man who at one time was powerful and handsome. It was filled with a faded confidence and the broken eyes of a fallen leader. His putrid rotting flesh made this thing, that was at one time a man, just like the tattered ancient rag that covered him. The rest of his clothes were also at one time fine and breath taking, but now were faded and threadbare. Wearing burgundy and grey, he stood there on the horizon staring at me. My eyes were drawn to the one thing that still gleamed with care that lay upon his chest. Somehow from the distance that was between us I was able to clearly make out a brooch that he wore over his heart. It was an oval with the image of a large stone half buried in the ground. The craftsmanship of this piece of jewelry far exceeded anything I had yet seen, save perhaps for the frightening countenance of Ukumog.

"I am not playing games. Who are you? Why are you attacking this city?"

Wracked

My mind drifted to the faces of the powerful men from my latest vision. Nearly fainting again as I recalled the power of it, I searched through them to find some piece of the puzzle that I was missing. In the circle of faces, far away from the pointy bearded commander, I recalled a face half covered in a delicate half mask made of burgundy colored silk. The charming and chiseled face of the older gentleman stood out among his peers. His facade was filled with apprehension and sadness.

"You know why I am here. I bring my men here because my lord wishes it. For no other reason. Am I to understand that you are to interfere?"

"Why would that concern you?"

His focus seemed to waver for a moment as he considered the situation. "The things we all do concern me, Wrack. Is this some sort of game, boy?"

"Game? Why would I play a game with you? I assume that you are the creature known as the Rotting One."

I felt his power was washing over me. He was poking my defenses looking for a weakness. A hatred grew in my chest and my blood began to boil with a cold fury. My teeth ground together as this anger and fury built inside me like a growing fire. I steeled myself against his perception and felt the cold pain from my spine shoot out to my finger tips and up into my eyes. My right hand longed for the handle of a blade. This wild part of my soul wished to charge through the men that formed the ocean between us and clash then and there upon the field. It wasn't his warmth I wanted, it was something far far darker. I wanted to feast upon his soul after I shattered its protective fleshy shell. Breathing heavily, I found it harder and harder not to let this insanity take over my body and

Chapter 9

let our two powers collide. Even deep in my hypnotic hatred, I felt Murks squirm in my pocket. "The Rotting One is attacking me, Master!"

"HEY!" I screamed, and with it went a lash of energy that struck the Rotting One. He reeled back as if he had been whipped across the face.

"Very well," he said as he brought it hand to his face. "You have made yourself abundantly clear. My duty has changed. Your reemergence has become more of a priority than crushing this pathetic servant of the Baron. When we meet again, you will answer for that attack." He turned and disappeared behind the siege engines.

"You ok, Murks?"

"Murks is ok, master. Thank you."

"No need to thank me, Murks."

"Master has never been this nice before."

Out in the field, there began the sound of trumpets calling. Some men started slowly retreating, yet some were driven on by their lust for battle. I jumped off the wall and into the city. Sprawling before me, the whole town was in a state of murderous looting and fires. This once dark and peaceful town was now anything but. Streets washed with blood, the hunger of the city's secret master evident on the face of all its denizens.

Setting off to find Brin and Avar I whispered, "I have a feeling that a lot of things are much different than they use to be, Murks. A lot of things."

Wracked

Chapter 10

My senses were overwhelmed with a blur of smoke and haunting screams. A few opportunists spied me walking through the messy riot. As they took their first step toward me, another flaming ball crashed into a nearby building. The resulting wind blew the threadbare tattered hood off my head. Upon seeing the mostly dead visage of my person, an approaching group reconsidered their intended violence toward me. One glare from my sunken eyes told them that I was not to be trifled with. They slid back into the cracks from which they had emerged.

Calling out for Avar and Brin proved useless. The noisy storm of greed and bloodlust swirling around me was far too loud for anyone to hear me. Taking a deep breath, I closed my eyes and tried to imagine where they were. At first it was impossible to shove the assaulting sounds from my mind, but slowly an angry calm came over me. My gut showed my mind which way to go, and I didn't question it. I just followed my instincts.

Almost immediately, I found myself slipping through the alleys and back streets of Yellow Liver. The violent chaos of the main streets masked a horrifying macabre world in the capillaries of the town. At first it was just streams of dark liquid pooling on the sides of the stone street. Soon there were fragments of previous living things laying strewn in small numbers. Like breadcrumbs

Wracked

leading the way, they grew in frequency and definition as I drew closer to where they were leading me. Undefinable masses of flesh became fingers, and fingers became feet until entire limbs or huge chunks of torsos were lying in the street or haphazardly handing from eaves. Disgust filled the back of my throat, but the smell of death hanging in the air and terrible indicators of a greater violence did not deter me from my path.

Turning a tight corner, I came face to face with at least six or seven ghouls. Stained from matted hair to their grimy feet with dark wet blood, they turned from their feeding frenzy to stare at me. I could not count how many bodies were in the pile they were all picking flesh from. It was a random pile of bloody torn meat with arms, legs, faces, and every imaginable part of human bodies lying in a massive heap. More ghouls appeared on the roof tops overhead, each with a fragment of humanity hanging from their salivating maws.

I wasn't afraid. These pathetic monsters were nothing but twisted dead people, controlled by a burning hunger for human flesh. Whatever it was that caused this state, I felt sorry for them. My pity became disgust as my thoughts drifted to the broken people on which they feasted. *Some of these bodies could have been their neighbors or family. Is there any piece of the person they were inside them? Do they weep in the secret prison of their corrupted forms for the innocent people they have slaughtered to feed their twisted hunger? Do they even realize what they are doing?* A growl began to rumble in the chest of one of the ghouls. It spread to the rest of them quickly enough. Bloody, gurgling growls filled the silent air. My angry calm was uninterrupted by their weak attempt to remove me from their feast. Instead, I saw the handle of a knife still clutched the hand of a dismembered arm in the pile.

Chapter 10

Smoothly, I moved down and pried the knife free of the dead fingers. Attempting to increase their failing intimidation, the growling became more aggressive. While hunched on all fours, one of them started scraping their leg against the stone street aggressively. Unconcerned, I examined the blade of the knife. The uneven edge of the blade was covered in nicks and pits. Stains from food long devoured decorated the sides. Worn leather covered a wooden handle below. I ignored the ghouls as they moved closer to surround me on the street and above.

"Good knife." I said to no one in particular. "Certainly looks like I has seen a fair share of use. Not a real weapon though, just a utensil. Something tells me though," my eyes met the closest ghoul, "that it could still split you open."

As if they were waiting for a cue, all the ghouls descended on me in a swarm of claws and teeth. The sounds of my robe and flesh tearing filled the dark pocket inside the mass of ghouls where I was now held. The pain of their attacks made the bitter cold grow inside me and soon the only sound I heard was the grinding of my own teeth.

There was no thinking, I just attacked. Jabbing and slashing with the blade in my hand, the knife collided with soft flesh and hard bone, over and over again. Cold, thick blood streamed over my hand. The mass of monsters that sounded me suddenly changed their tactic. Claws began grasping at my arms and legs and it was all I could do to slip from them. Pushing forward, I was able to break out of the circle of ghouls that were scrambling over each other to come at me. The entire group of them came crashing down and tossed here and there as I turned to face them. A few of the close ones began a chorus of hissing. Their sudden change of behavior confused me for a moment. The arrival of two new enemies woke me from my stupor: glistening, shadowy dog-shaped creatures with human eyes floating in the viscous fluid mass of their bodies. The ghouls began a sickly laugh as the dogs padded into the alleyway, stopping a short distance away. Their lips curled back to reveal human-like teeth in their canine jaws. Thick black drool escaped one of the dog's mouth and each drop let a small stream of smoke drift upwards as it sizzled slightly when it met the stone.

"Oh, uzk."

They leapt at me with preternatural speed, leaving me only time to try and crouch defensively. Teeth dug into my arm and one of my legs, causing a burning pain. Screaming, I felt the cold within me being drained away. I pulled against them, struggling to pull my limbs free. The knife in my free hand swung wildly, cutting into the thick wet form of the dogs resulting in no change in my situation. The small amount of life that fueled my dead body was being drained away and I could do nothing to stop it. Slowly, my struggling slowed and the ghouls began to hover over the scene, mocking me with their gurgling laughter. The few that I had wounded kept their distance, clutching their wounds.

Rustling from inside my shredded robes led to the emergence of Murks from his hidden pocket. Standing on my chest I saw him nod at me with a calm certainty that only a creature with small indentions for a face could express. The muscles in my neck relaxed as more of my life was stolen, making my head crack against the stone.

"Kanderia hemograndata!" exclaimed the tiny voice I knew was Murks. One wet popping sound was followed by several more and a sloshing slurping noise filled the air. The smell of blood drifted to my nostrils and I welcomed it in. The two tiny feet pressing against my chest quickly became much heavier and I summoned all my strength to lift my head to see what was happening.

Chapter 10

Where the tiny Murks had once stood was now a much larger hemodan. The surface of his normally clumpy form was now more fluid and malleable, it was churning and changing. Something sharp pierced through my chest right where Murks stood, and within seconds his hands ignited with steaming dark power.

In complete darkness I was drowning. Something wet and thick was forcing its way into my burning lungs. Pressure from the soft but strong matter crushing me seemed like it was trying to pry its way into my eyes. Nothing but a muffled whimper appeared when I tried to scream. My body began to twist in the tensing mass. *There's no point. I can't escape.* Surrendering to my fate, I let it in. As my body relaxed and stopped fighting it, all the openings in my head were invaded. Eyelids peeled back, mouth opened, nostrils breeched, ears violated. This dark stalker had won.

Violent vibrations wracked the mass around me and a bone shaking scream was let loose from many unseen mouths. The grip on me loosened and the invasion of my skull came to an end. Light pushed back the shiny dark forms, revealing me like the pit in the center of a peach. The source of the light drew closer and drove the thing away, as all the while it protested with eardrum bursting screams.

My thoughts were too muddy to realize what was going on. In the light I saw my hands. They were young and alive. Gasping for air I felt relief and gratitude. The source of light stared at me with the flickering eye of a lantern. Behind it was a small cast of silhouettes. The one holding the lantern stepped forward and touched me.

"Are you alright?"

Wracked

In a flash I was looking into wizened, grey eyes. They were filled with an urgent sadness. They were filled with betrayal. The flesh around the eye twitched and like a predator I sensed fear. The right eye gave birth to a single tear. Looking down I saw a nasty black iron sword impaled in the chest of the old man. His beard and robes soaked with blood. It was my hand on the handle of the sword and for a moment I felt a rage subside. The kind of satisfying feeling that only the quenched lust for revenge or power can bring. Gasping and stepping back, I couldn't form any words.

This isn't me! I didn't do this! How did this happen? I should be there, in the woods! But the woods around us were empty, as was the field where the bodies of the children and their murderers should have been. A sting in my eyes brought forth a waterfall of tears and my throat filled with acid. It was me in the twisted armor and my hands were covered in blood.

The old man stood there with his hands bound, his chest impaled, and unwilling to die with one single tear exploring the wrinkles between his eye and his chin. His eyes filled with disappointment and betrayal. Opening his mouth to speak, he paused. I saw his eyebrow quiver, and the weak face became steel.

Grief weakened my knees and I fell into the bloody mud. My sobs cried out for forgiveness, but fell upon stone and found no purchase.

"I did this for you, yet you squandered my gift. You gave in to them."

His words might as well have cut out my tongue, as the resulting guilt certainly rendered me unable to speak. Unworthy of looking him in the face, I started at the blood on the ground. In it, I could see a thousand lives lost because of my failure to act. My weakness. Among them, all those who meant anything to me. While I did not know their names or remember their faces, I felt the

Chapter 10

vast emptiness that their passage left within my heart. Not able to take it any longer, I closed my eyes. Entire jaw quivering, I forced my mouth to whisper, "Grandfather?"

Opening my eyes again, the tears had dried and I was again in black robes. Before me on the cold marble floor was a stone bowl filled with ashes. Implements of ritual were around the bowl. A knife, candles, incense, a fine glass filled with clear water, and a roll of parchment covered in scribbling.

"Well?" said the deep mocking voice of the commander. "Shall we begin this? Se'Naat, your boy seems a little distracted. Perhaps we can do your silly magic at some other time."

"No brother, we must do this now. This war must end and the only way to do so is through this...connection," came a familiar, smug voice.

Sneaking glances at the commander, I saw him laughing to the people near him. To his left was a stern looking man in ivory and green robes. The white space was filled with subtle silver designs sewn into the fabric. Just above his young, strong face was a crown made of gold and silver strands twisted into elegant knots. The strands came together in the front and held aloft a large oval shaped emerald which glistened in the light of the chamber. To the commander's right was a confident older man, his salt and pepper hair partially covered by a burgundy silk mask which tightly covered half his face. Lurking in the shadows behind these three powerful men was the shifty form of a man with long, stringy hair, wearing a leather harness filled with daggers. A shameful hunger lingered behind his empty face.

There was a slight tug deep inside my chest. Confused, I tried to find the source of this discomfort and found nothing there. Again the tug came, deeper was the sensation this time and with the discomfort came a strange pain. There was a pause between

Wracked

tugs just long enough for me to panic, but not long enough for me to seek help from the people around me. So strong was the tug that followed that it felt as if my soul were being drawn out through an invisible barbed thread running out my chest. Breathing heavy, I clawed at my chest. Silently I screamed for help between gasping for air. My company in the large chamber paid me no heed and the world became dark. Alone and afraid, my head pounded and a cold horrible rage filled my empty soul. Broiling inside me, the pain of my anger pushed at every wall within me until it found escape by forcing my eyes open.

Wracked with burning cold pain, I gasped for air as I watched the purple smoke rise from my eyes. Still panicked and filled with anger, I felt no pain, but paranoia forced me to look around before I moved. On my chest was a crumpled, lumpy ball about the size of my fist. Fearful, I quickly sat up and caught the ball in my hand. "Murks?! Murks, say something!" Expecting the tiny voice to enter my head, I waited. The ball was his little scabby form, curled into a ball. His form now completely dry and back to his original size. Turning him over in my hands, I looked for even the smallest sign of life. "Murks!"

All around us lay broken and slightly charred bodies of the ghouls. The proximity of their forms made it look like they had been pushed away from where I lay by some great explosion. Signs of such an explosion was even evident on the buildings in the alley, but in their condition a little more damage was almost unnoticeable. "We are safe now Murks. Murks, whatever you did, you saved us. Murks! Wake up Murks!" This was all my fault.

Chapter 10

If I hadn't been so lost, so weak, I could have prevented this. I could have stopped the attack on the town. I could have saved the children and never lost Brin and Avar. I can't be weak. I have to be strong. The image of the old man's disapproving eyes filled my mind and I felt my jaw clench. *I didn't kill you, old man. That commander did. It wasn't my fault. I was just a boy.* This didn't stop the tearful betrayed look in my mind. *I DIDN'T KILL YOU!* Tightened fists collided with the stone street. My frustration vented through a scream from the deepest part of my gut. Anger drove me to my feet, and while still yelling, I smashed my bare fists against the walls of the buildings. I focused on one support beam for the building and began a barrage of punches, trying to push the rage out from my soul through my fists. "I don't even know who I am! How you can you hold me to this impossible standard!? Stop haunting me! Visions, memories, ghosts! To the pit with you! Get! Out! Of! My! Head!" Each word was punctuated with violence. The support of the building I was letting loose on was cracking beneath my assault and with the final word, the bones in my fist broke and sawed their way through my skin. Crying, I felt to the ground. Seeing Murks on the ground next to me, I cradled him in my hands and wept.

I could feel my shattered hand repairing itself and unlike before, there was no comfort in my immortality. In my heart, I cursed this cruel fate. Haunted by images and insecurity, I hated my situation, I hated myself. Just as I began wishing I had never woken at that accursed waterfall, I felt a stirring in my hands. The rage and sadness were replaced instantly with hope. With wide eyes I opened my hands. "Murks?"

"Master," he whispered. "Murks saved us. Can Murks sleep for a while now, Master?"

Wracked

The acid in my throat turned to sweet sugar. A smile claimed my face, and I couldn't stop the little laugh that escaped it. "Sure, Murks. You can sleep all you like." I slid him into his hidden pocket and wiped away the grey tears from the edges of my eyes. "I really need to do something about these robes. They really are nothing but shreds." In my mind, I felt the little hemodan agree with me, before he drifted off to sleep.

The alley had become quiet. Echoes of the war going on in the streets surrounding it spilled in over the roofs and around the corners. For a brief moment, I enjoyed the simple peace before heading back out into the mess to find my lost friends.

Much of the city was on fire. The commotion in the street hadn't really died down, but it had a completely different tone. Looting had all but stopped. Now people were running from a combination of ghouls and the glistening shadow creatures. Dark skinless dogs chased people through the streets. Spiders made of a ball of tar for a body and black finger bones attached to form the legs wrapped human-sized cocoons. I darted in and out of the street trying not to be seen by any of the host of hungry monsters which were running amok in the streets.

"Brin! Avar! Brin! Avar!" If they were answering my call, I couldn't hear them.

A pack of ghouls went charging off away from where I was. Thinking that maybe they had seen me, and were running to get help, I decided to follow them. With powerful ease, they used every surface available to them to lope their way to their destination. Unable to do the same thing, I lost them when they went over a roof as a group.

"Uzk. Uzkin' ghouls." Then I noticed how quiet this part of the city was. All the noise seemed so far away. *Oh uzk, is this an ambush?* Carefully, I stepped out of the open and tried to quietly

Chapter 10

follow the direction that the ghouls had gone. Cutting through an alley, I found myself in a whole different section of the city. Compared to the rest of it, this place seemed nice and clean. The buildings were not quite as narrow and there was not the sense that they might fall over at any moment. The stones in the street were all cleanly placed in the ground, and there was not much filth crusted to the sides of it. Even the air felt a little clearer.

Continuing my search, I found myself quietly walking through a well kept courtyard when I heard some yelling and the clashing of steel. Smoke drifted through the courtyard from outside like fast moving earthly clouds. *Where is the ambush?* My guard started to drop. The walls and manor surrounding the courtyard were obviously once elegant. Even with its age and disrepair, it had an air of importance and authority. I tried to imagine the place in the height of its glory, with well groomed gardens and pristine plaster walls, bright blooming flowers nourished by the bright sun and the laughter of the children playing around them. *Have I been here before?* My daydreaming of a foreign life was interrupted by a distant cry of "UZK!"

Abandoning my stealth, I charged towards the voice. The closer I came, the clearer the noises were. Sprinkled in with the cries were the sounds of metal on metal and metal on flesh. Gurgling and horrible wet roaring was the next texture to be added. Then it came. "Avar! Here come more of them, pull back in with me!" My hopes had become reality. The voice was Brin's.

The next layer of sound was the simple accent of the breathing and grunting that people do in battle. Brin's grunt sounded more like curse words without form and Avar was just venting exhaustion. There were other voices there with them too, for once they didn't seem against my two friends. As I stepped around the corner of the large house I saw, them, a horde of clawing

Wracked

ghouls tearing at the center of their circle that contained just a few people. Avar's tall lanky form stood above the rest, his blond hair looking almost silver in the moonlight. To his side Brin's dark hair was as active in attacking the air as were her two swords, cleaving both ghoul flesh and the very air around her. Two other helmeted heads were in the circle with them. Helmets that had the black iron look of the city guard. When closed the distance halfway to them, one of the guards was pounced upon by some of the swirling around them. Screaming and struggling, he tried to break free of their hungry grip to no avail. Within seconds he had been pulled from the protective circle and out into the frenzy. Parts of his armor and person began flying through the air as the ghouls peeled their tasty reward. The circle drew tighter as the three remaining people stepped in to fill the now empty space.

"HEY!" I shouted.

All faces turned to me as if lightning had just struck where I stood. Allowing her defenses to drop for one moment, Brin saw me and let me have one of her hidden warm smiles. The hair on my body stood up, and I felt the cold pain race through my spine. The sound of battle crashed again in the courtyard as the onslaught continued. A handful of ghouls detached themselves from the main attack and came at me, some of them on all fours, others just loping toward me with a painful and awkward-looking yet surprising speed. Trails of bloody drool sprayed into the air from their gaping maws. Pain and hate shut my jaw tightly and my feet planted where they were. I wanted to become a wall for these creatures to crash into at such a speed that they would be pulverized into lifeless goo. I wanted to sear them and cut them into tiny bits with dark fire from the pits of my eyes. I wanted to break them under my powerful fist. Like a vice my jaw squeezed my teeth together. Some of them screamed out as if they were on the verge of shattering.

Chapter 10

Air rushed around my ankles and fluttered my robes toward the oncoming ghouls. Undaunted, their slavering charge continued. The unkempt grass in the yard there bent to the will of the waves of air rushing past them, but I saw that the current of it was not reaching to the main cluster of the combat. Stinging pain entered my fingers and suddenly I felt as if the wind were a puppet and I its master. An evil smirk floated to the surface of my face as if it had lain beneath the surface and was just now revealed. I had no time to question the seeming free will of my expressions; instead, I ended the smirk by forcing all my rage, all my frustration, all my hunger into a bellowing howl that erupted from my body, causing my entire body to tense.

No recognition of my actions registered in the eyes of my assailants. They kept coming in what seemed like slow motion, while behind them I saw the air solidify. The rage expelled from me seemed to form another wall in front of me. Still exhaling all my hate and with tears streaming from my unblinking eyes, I pulled back with my fingers which themselves were cascading with tiny bolts of electric dark. The wall of air and the wall of malice raced silently towards each other within a blink of an eye. There was an explosion of dark bloody mush and a rain of tiny wet bits, and they were gone.

When my muscles relaxed, they surged with the gritty sweetness of honey. I breathed, exhaling air that felt like fire. The skirmish before me still raged with the three still in the center. More of the ghouls lay on the ground, either twitching away their final moments, whining like a dog with a mortal wound, or completely still. Being both exhausted and pumping with energy, I ran forward into the cloud of ghouls that still harassed my friends not knowing if they had seen the gruesome spectacle just moments before.

Wracked

With no understanding or control of whatever power I had, I charged unarmed into the fray. Shoving, punching, and kicking, I fought my way through the stinky, foul beasts. I distracted one long enough that Brin was able to bring Ukumog down on its shoulder, and pulled free when the wound had been opened nearly to the center of its chest. Wailing, it fell into a bloody heap. Joining the three, I continued to fearlessly stand against our foes, my companions carefully striking each time a target became within range.

"Who is your friend?" The standing guard asked.

"Oh, this is Wrack, like a spice rack. Spicy, meet Matthew."

"Greetings, Matthew. Unusual for me to be on the same side with the guard," I said, wishing I could glare at Avar who was behind me in the circle.

Matthew parried a ghoul's attack deftly, "Yeah, not sure there really is a guard anymore, to be honest. When the ghouls crawled out of the sewers, the whole place went mad."

"So, you knew about the monsters living under you and you still followed uzkin' orders?" Brin chimed in with her usual charm.

Matthew was silent for a moment. "Can't say I had much of a choice." He stepped forward to slash at one of the ghouls as they attacked. The enemies on either side of that ghoul also lunged forward and opened Matthew's face.

"NO!" Avar dived in front of him with his shield preventing him from being dragged into the darkness beyond.

"Showed up at the right time, Wrack. Things are looking a bit grim," Brin said.

"Look on the bright side, Brin. This way we can all be eaten together."

Another ghoul lunged at us and Ukumog ended the connection between the attacking arm and the body.

Chapter 10

"When you fell off that wall, I thought you were a goner for sure. Somethin' told me though. I hadn't seen the last of you."

"If you two haven't noticed, it is now three and a half against, like, fifteen. Could you please save the flirting for later?" Avar's voice was filled with frustration and worry.

With Matthew protected in the middle of us, we three held back the tide of hungry monsters.The ghoul's eyes all betrayed them. This silly game of keeping us in the middle had ceased to be amusing. Any moment they were going to all pounce us at once. I felt Brin tense right next to me. She knew it was coming, too.

"Get ready, fellas."

A few near me crouched back, ready to leap when suddenly there was a gurgling howl nearby which turned the heads of nearly all the ghouls. Avar and I used this moment to further prepare for the eventual attack. Brin and Ukumog had other plans. The moment their heads were turned, metal and blood began to fly as she cut a hole through their line. I tried to move with her, just used to her leading us through fights this way.

From behind us Avar's voice changed the situation. "Matthew is still alive! We can't leave him!"

"Uzk." Brin muttered under her breath. We prepared to return to Avar who was standing over the fallen guard. Matthew was doing his best to fight them off, but the wounds on his face were making just seeing anything difficult.

There was a gurgling howl that came in response to the first one from somewhere else. Then another and another. A stream of ghouls started leaving to follow the sounds. Brin caught a few of them before they were able to leave, but very quickly we were left in the yard on our own. The tangled wreckage had more forms with guard armor and livery, telling me that this battle had started out with many more on both sides.

Wracked

"Did we win?" Matthew strained to ask.

"Nah. Something called them off."

"That's worrisome."

"Yeah." Avar watched as the ghouls left. The desire to purge them all burning in his eyes.

One final ghoul went running past us in the courtyard and with it came the sound of a child crying. As he left our proximity, I saw the crying girl hanging upside down and sideways from its arms. They were gone before any of us could do anything, but that didn't stop Avar from trying to chase it.

"Drop that girl!" He shouted, but they were already gone.

"Avar. Avar. I know where they are going." Each moment Matthew's voice became more labored. "There is an entrance to the sewers that way. Go there. That is where the children are being held."

"You're coming with us, Matt. We need you."

"Sorry, Avar. Don't think I am gunna be able to go." He coughed up blood as he gave a little laugh. "Sure is something though."

Tears formed in Avar's eyes. "What?"

"Fighting without fear. Not fear of death, but fear of them. If I had ever known how that felt, I woulda done a lot of things differ—" Coughing up more blood moved quickly into his body twitching and his eyes rolling back into his head. And he was gone.

"Matthew?" Avar's sorrow began escaping in sobs, and in moments he was crying. Even Brin seemed affected by Matthew's death, her flexing chin exposing the grief hidden behind her steely face.

His face pointed at the moon Avar, said with no rage or malice, "Why must all the brave ones die? We need good hearted people like him. I don't understand. How can we defeat them, when

Chapter 10

our enemy cares about nothing? Standing against such malice is like trying to catch the roaring wind in a storm. I...I can't catch the wind."

This outpouring of emotion over someone he barely knew was so alien to me. Searching my short life, my dreams, my nightmares, I could find nothing. Nothing except Brin. *What would happen to me if she were to die like this? Would I even care?* I hoped I would never have to answer that question.

Wracked

Chapter 11

"Avar, we need to get the uzk out of here before those things come back."

He ignored her, still consumed by his grief.

"Matthew is gone, Avar. That little girl needs our help. She needs YOUR help. Who knows how long they will keep her? Each second we stay is one closer to when they tear her apart."

Immediately he stopped crying. He sniffed back his leaking tears a few times, then picked up his shield and mace. "Ok. Lets go crush some of these uzkers."

"Woo! Now you are talking my language!" She darted off in front of us, as usual, towards the place where Matthew had said the entrance was.

Fire spread to this part of town. The sky was aglow with orange light. Echoing screams and sounds of fighting got closer and closer as we left the decaying beauty of the manor behind. Before it disappeared into the twisting narrow streets, I looked back at the dark beams and white plaster walls of the manor house. *Yet another question unanswered.*

The violent chaos of the streets faded away into a despairing madness. Loved ones of the half eaten and slaughtered hid everywhere. Their disjointed grief echoed the pain that was hidden behind Avar's purposeful steps. The fallout of this war was heartbreaking, but I felt no sympathy. *You are just as much a monster as they are, ya know. Once these ghouls are gone, you're next.* I hated myself for being so unfeeling, for being this monster that I was, and I didn't even know who or what that was.

Swift moving shadows loped toward the same direction we were going. This quickened Avar's pace, and soon he was leading us through the streets.

"What was all that back there?" I asked.

Brin shrugged, "Dunno. I think they were old friends or something. Before the fight started, there was some talk like they knew each other."

Her statements increased my concern that Avar might do something careless. We needed to remain focused at the job ahead. There was no way we could kill The Ghoul, the lord of this drooling insanity. He was one of the Doomed, and according to Avar, impossible to kill. Secretly I sent a wish out into the sky above me that he wouldn't do anything stupid to satiate his pain.

Spotting some dark trails stained into the stone, Avar followed them. Even with the grief I knew he still felt, his instincts were right on. Quickly, we found a hole in the side of an old building. The stench of sewer and rot became overwhelming as we drew closer in. Regardless of the sickening stink, we pressed on through the awkward crack.

Avar's head tilted up towards the moon. With a sad smile he started speaking out loud, "Ssli'Garion. Mother of inspiration. Matron of purity. Protect your servant in his time of need. We head into the lair of one of those Doomed by your most sacred prophecy. We do so to prevent the shedding of innocent blood. Too much blood has found its way into the silver forest. We must end this

Chapter 11

tidal wave of evil. Lady, be with us now and let your light cast out the ever twisting secret darkness." He took a deep breath and then stepped inside.

Just inside was a hole in the floor. The stone and dirt were wet with ichor and blood. Debris of corpses and clothing lay thrown around the hole to form a macabre drain, all piles slanted toward the disgusting maw. Any thought of turning back was shattered when a child's crying voice echoed up from below.

"Let's go. I am going first." Removing his pack, he moved in and started climbing down before either of us could argue with him. Likewise, Brin shed her non-combat gear and made sure that Ukumog was firmly attached to its belt. As soon as Avar completely disappeared into the darkness below, Brin followed. I stood alone at the top for a moment listening to the wailing of strangers floating in through the hole. Bracing myself against the horrors I knew I was about to face, I followed my two friends into the tunnels below Yellow Liver.

Avar splashed down into a stagnant river of filth. There was a strange ambient light which allowed for all of us to make out shapes and forms around us. Wanting to see more, I turned my eyes to dark sight. What I saw made me glad my friends could not see as I did. The tunnel was caked with gore. The mason work of the stone tunnel was mostly hidden by a layer of scabs, as if the tunnel itself were wounded. In the fluid in which we stood floated both human waste and decayed human parts. Vermin also scuttled away from us in the forms of rats and insects. Nothing about this place was inviting, and I could not imagine what kind of sentient creature could make this place their home, especially an immortal with tremendous power.

Wracked

Brin seemed to sense Avar's hesitation. After waiting for a moment, she led the way. Picking one direction of the two available, we started quietly moving our way deeper in.

"How are we going to find our way out?"

"I dunno yet, Avar. I'm figuring this out as we move along, just like you."

As we moved away from the entrance, the tunnel grew darker. The faint glow of Ukumog was our only light. *Clink!* It was free from the belt and held out in front.

"Uzk. I can't see gaak in here."

"I can."

"Whoa, yeah. Your eyes are glowing again and stuff. Why don't you lead then?"

"I don't have a weapon, Brin. You stay in front, and I will guide you."

I moved from third position to second. Using my hands on her sides, we quickly worked out a smooth way for me to guide her through the tunnel. Clutching onto the shreds of my robe, Avar held up his shield and protected the rear. Slowly, we shuffled our way through filth and decay.

The maze of tunnels under the street was a decent reflection of the city on the surface, winding and twisting narrow tunnels with walls that loomed in close. At many places it seemed like the whole place could cave in at any moment. Each time we reached an intersection of tunnels, I used the gore as my guide. Each scab-covered wall would lead us to another and another. Walking in that muck was difficult. There was a thick layer of something mushy that had settled on the bottom, and sometimes our feet would collide with solid objects that none of us wanted to reach down and see. We just hoped it wasn't something that was going to bite.

Chapter 11

The idea of the place being trapped had crossed my mind, but seeing as Avar's normal paranoia had returned, I didn't think it a good idea to mention. Even with daylight, it would have taken us hours to progress through here examining every inch for suspicious things. With the darkness, the terrible design, and the grim decor it would be easy to hide gruesome traps.

Hours passed in the tunnels. "Are you sure we are going the right way?"

"No. No I am not, Avar. If I could give you my eyes so you could lead us, I would."

This exchange would happen every ten to fifteen minutes. No matter what I said, it would not quiet his anxiety. My feet were cold and numb. Brin and Avar began to slow down from exhaustion and insecurity. After that long in the dark, I was not sure I could lead us back to the surface, even if we finished what we came to do in here. *What about what the Shadow said? Will the master of Yellow Liver know me?* Trying to push thoughts from my mind, I continued to push forward.

The gore on the walls started to become less and less frequent and I started to grow concerned about the direction we were heading. Just about the time I was about to suggest that we turn around, I heard voices, low whispering from in front of us. With each sloshing step the sounds grew louder, and the runes on Ukumog got brighter.

"Something is up ahead."

"Lemme get up there, Brin, and I can block the hallway to protect you."

After moving Avar up front, block the tunnel they did. Avar's shield took up half the tunnel all by itself, and thirsty edge of Ukumog waited quietly on the other. The whispering got louder

Wracked

then stopped. For a second I thought I heard some from behind us, but I dismissed it as just an echo. Squinting my eyes to see further into the darkness ahead, all looked ok. Then, movement.

"Uh. Here they come!"

"How many?!"

"Lots."

"Gaak. I am ready. Come get me, you uzkers! Ukumog is going to love the taste of you!"

Shouting names that ghouls don't know at them did not prove to be a useful deterrent. They came barreling down the tunnel. The first few crashed into Avar's shield. I had to brace his back to keep him up. Dim blue trails swirled up, down, around, and back as Brin put Ukumog to use. Gurgled screams and howls echoed down the tunnel and through the tunnels beyond.

"Well, they know we are here now."

"Bah. These things just don't know how to die quiet."

On the other side of my two friends was a machine of death. The ghouls were throwing themselves at our weapons with suicidal fury. With the sheer number of opponents, there seemed to be no hope of survival. Moments later, the cunning of our enemies was revealed.

Claws gashed my back. Screaming in surprise and pain, I turned to see another host of ghouls behind me.

"Uh oh."

"What?" Brin asked without looking back.

Another ghoul lunged at me. At the last second I grabbed his claw, but his face kept coming at me. With my free hand, I snatched him by the neck and slammed his head into the stone wall next to me. It exploded like a melon being hit by a hammer and his body fell limp.

"More back here!" I shouted.

Chapter 11

Brin responded, "Little busy on this side."

"Uh—" Another one charged at me. I brought up my boot spraying a trail of filthy water behind it. My foot collided with the ghoul's jaw, and the forces combined caused a very satisfying crunching noise from the bones in his face. The crowd behind him did not seem persuaded to stop. "Could use a little help back here!"

"Avar, help him with that shield!"

"This shield is the only thing keeping you alive!"

Two more ghouls came at me. They dodged under my attempt to bring my fist backwards against them. The first one ripped my chest, the other grabbed my arm and chomped down on me with its unholy maw.

"AAGGGGGG! GUYS!" Numbing cold flashed to my hands like a wave of electricity. Palming the head of the one who clawed me, I smashed its face directly into the back of the other one's head, crushing my arm on the other side. Purple lightening arced through both of them, causing a waft of clean smelling air before filling the sewer with the stink of burnt flesh. Both bodies fell into the sewer soup below and the lightening flickered on my crushed and wounded arm, healing the wounds.

Without turning around, Avar asked, "What was that light? What the uzk is going on back there?"

"Nothing. Just keep fighting."

Heat was leaving my eyes in waves. I felt it drift upwards over my brow and into the air over my head. The remaining host of ghouls stared at me, not sure what to do next. The power was coursing through me so strongly that I drifted to act solely on instinct. Curling my hands into claw-like bowls I spread them to either side of my body. Purple tongues of lightning licked at my fingers and large strikes shot back and forth from my hands. Rage, hatred, and disdain swelled within me. *These things must die.* The

Wracked

flow of power was now arcing between my hands and swirling with black energy. Turning my palms toward the tunnel, I let the anger loose, and with a screaming bellow, the dark power blew down the tunnel in a wave, disintegrating all the ghouls it touched as it went. The force of unleashing the wave pushed me back against my wall of defenders behind me.

"You ok?" Brin asked.

Out of breath I responded, "I think I am ok."

"Thank the Lady, we scared them away!" Avar celebrated.

"I think they were more afraid of Ukumog than they are of some Lady who lives on the moon."

"Shattup." Avar grinned at her. "Oh look! Spicy got some too! Good work buddy!" He indicated the few ghouls which lay floating in the filth at my feet.

"Yeah. I managed."

Sarcastic camaraderie even here in the darkest of places. I was glad to be back with them, yet they seemed completely unaware of the power growing in me. *Best not to worry them.* Before long we were moving again. This time I was following more than just the gore on the walls. There was something deep in my chest that was pulling me. Not unlike the presence I felt on the battlefield, I sensed something here. It was like that night at the warehouse, but so much stronger.

"Gah. This place stinks. How could anyone live in this filth!?" Avar whispered, as if we were all not aware of the stench of both sewage and decay that filled all of our noses.

Brin grimaced, "Quit being a baby, Avar." I could tell that the smell was bothering her as well.

"Here, use this to cover your nose and mouth," I said as I tore pieces of my robe and handed it to each of them.

Chapter 11

Avar thanked me and quickly tied the fabric around his face. From his eyes I could tell that the smell of the dirt and age of my clothes were only slightly better than the stench that surrounded us.

Forging on through the darkness it was hard to tell if we were even moving in the right direction, but I let the pulling force lead me. I kept thinking about the Shadow's words about the Ghoul, and how he said that I would know him when he saw me, but like most things the shadow said, I didn't fully understand.

"This way," Brin whispered bringing me out of my thoughts. She moved into a passage at a fork that seemed covered in darker and more viscous ichor than the rest of the slimy tunnels. It was then that my vision saw the scratch marks on the walls.

It looked as if hundreds of fingernails had been dragged along the sides of the walls. When I looked up, I saw the reason for the dark ichor. The ceiling had been patched with the gnawed bones of all manner of creatures. This was unlike the other gore that was smeared in places. It seemed as if someone were rebuilding the tunnels with this gore. I guess I stopped moving for a moment, because Avar tried to look through the darkness to see what I was staring at, and Brin turned around and whispered, "What is it?" in my direction.

"Nothing," I lied and kept following her. I could feel fear in the back of my throat, the same feeling I had when I saw Brin tied to the chair in the cellar in Yellow Liver. I looked at her through the darkness and at that moment realized that I couldn't lose her, this woman whose gruff exterior held within it someone as complex and damaged as myself. Someone, who for whatever reason, had grown attached to my enigma. In her own way, she knew that she was tied to the fate of the Doomed. I knew that whatever happened when we found the Ghoul, I could not let her die.

Wracked

Light was reflecting off the walls and the wet filth beneath our feet. Flickering as it was, I could tell it was torch or firelight from a chamber up ahead. Brin and Avar drew their weapons. Off the belt, Ukumog was humming slightly. I still wasn't sure how I was going to help. Whatever power it was that lingered inside me, I had little to no control over it. I thought about the children from the hovels, trapped with the Ghoul, waiting. Waiting for a horrible death being eaten alive. My mind turned to the broken families above us and to the one brave child who had sat near me at the gate. As before, I felt a burning chill awaken within my hands. In the darkness I could see the dark purple energy rising like steam off my exposed skin.

Around the corner we went. The sickening noises of meat being pulled from bones and a disgusting mouth messily slurping the marrow from those bones quietly roared its way down to us. Brin stopped and motioned for us to stay and remain silent. I knew she could see into the room that was just around the bend. I could see in her face that she was planning our attack, assessing the situation.

Avar shifted to look behind us, even though he couldn't see through the darkness. His armor collided with the stone wall making a scratching noise which seemed louder than thunder. Brin ducked back slightly bumping into me. I could feel the warmth of her body against mine and my desire for her warmth overwhelmed my desire to save the children. Somehow this stopped the cold energy that was coming from my arms, but I was too distracted to notice.

The noises from up ahead continued at a steady pace. We all came to the conclusion that we hadn't been heard. Brin moved forward and I followed. Avar, on the other hand, had looked up over his head, and found the skull of a child looking down at him,

Chapter 11

with one eye hanging from the socket and the skin of its face only half chewed off. Shock and horror overtook him, and he started scrambling away from it, his armored shoulders and mace banging and scraping against the stone echoed down the hallway. I turned around just in time to have him collide with me and knock me into the mix of sewage and filth at our feet. The splash was loud and it also carried down the tunnel.

"Oh uzk," was all Brin had to say.

An unearthly roar came down the tunnel at us like a wall of sound. I could almost see the skin of my companions crawling. Avar was still shaken by the sight of the ceiling. The roar didn't help him. He let out a cry, which was the final clue that whatever was in the chamber ahead of us had company.

Brin decided to move forward into the chamber. Avar hesitated and followed her while motioning for me to get out of the muck that he had knocked me into.

The room was filled with cages constructed with sinew and bones. The back of the room had a chair that was also made of gruesome materials, with a mat of torn clothes as the cushion. The floor and chair were soaked in blood. Weeping could be heard all around the room. Pitiful sounds were coming from the various cages of which only half were full.

"Tell the Baron I am only protecting what is mine," said a voice which echoed in the room and sent shivers down my spine. Brin cautiously stepped further into the room, trying to find where the voice came from.

"The Rotting One moves in on me, and his lordship sends me no aid. How else am I to fight him and his master if not by calling upon the power?" he continued to plead.

Wracked

Many of the caged children saw Avar and Brin and began reaching their tiny arms through the bars of their macabre cages in a plea for rescue from a fate which that had been forced to witness, for the bloody remains which lay strew around the room that had previously been their friends and family. Even Brin's hard exterior started to become overwhelmed with the horror of this place. Sympathy for the children could almost be seen welling up within her normally callous eyes. Avar was completely dumbfounded and was at a complete loss for how next to act.

Back in the tunnel, I was climbing out of the muck. The realization came that the power had ceased to flow from my arms. I tried to focus and bring it back. I kept trying to bring to mind the children, in particular, the curious child who was unafraid of me. Nothing seemed to make the power manifest. Lingering where I could see in the room, I impotently remained in the shadows.

Brin continued to move forward into the room, while Avar stepped over to the nearest cage which contained children. He started looking for a way to get them out. The children, in desperation, started crying and clawing at Avar's clothes.

"Tell the master that I am not calling forth the hidden ones to overthrow him. Doubtless, I am only trying to defend myself," the voice continued to whine.

Stopping near the middle of the circular room, Brin could still not see where the voice was coming from. Now expecting an attack from surprise, she tightened her grip on her sword. She turned slowly around trying to further examine the dark corners and hidden places behind the cages. The whining voice grew silent. Avar ceased his search to free the children and armed his mace and shield. He turned and also started scanning with his eyes for the origins of the voice.

Chapter 11

A few moments of silence filled the room before the voice spoke again. "You aren't from my master, are you? Doubtless you would be wearing his symbol. Who are you? Assassins from the King no doubt."

"We serve no Doomed King nor Baron, neither," said Avar valiantly. "Show yourself, coward."

"Cowardice is all in perception, moon-child. Doubtless you are a tasty one, no? I can taste your fear. It sours the meat in such a delicious way. Brave to mention the names of the Doomed. False courage to cloak the fear? Vanity is sweet and tender is the meat of those who wear the armor of justice, but never raise the sword. You, moon-child, shall remind me of meals lost to my memories of a fallen age. I will savor every chew, and make sure I drink all of your sweet fluids."

The imagery had the desired effect on Avar. He was visibly trembling, but still trying to be brave for the children in the cage who he was still trying to shield. Brin followed the voice with her eyes. Looking at the tall ceiling of the chamber, she could see bodies hanging from chains, most of them headless. Her sight caught one which retained its head and her eyes met the large cloudy marbles which were its eyes.

"Ceiling!" She called out which caused Avar's gaze to travel upward.

Graceful and frightening like a practiced predator, the Ghoul leapt from his chain perch on the ceiling where he had been hanging upside down and fell towards Avar. There was a loud clash and a rattle as Ghoul and shield collided, knocking Avar back into the cage behind him. The Ghoul's claws tore at the top of the shield, and he clung to it like a spider. The new weight of the shield caused Avar to fall to the ground. Pinned like prey under the shield and his attacker, it was all Avar could do to try and hide under the protection of the shield as an onslaught of quick attacks came from the dark form above him. Avar's other hand rose and his mace smashed into the side of the Ghoul, who let out a slight howl of surprise, but continued to try and get at Avar's throat.

Charging across the room, Brin held Ukumog aloft and swung down on the back of the predator. The swing left a blur of blue sheen and darkness in its wake. As it cut into the back of the Ghoul, it burst into life with dark energy. Intense blue light danced on the runic sides of the blade like I had never before seen. The same deep, whiny voice let loose an unearthly wail, and the Ghoul leapt from his prey back atop some of the cages. Sick-smelling greenish ooze dripped from the wound and was both on the floor and the sword from the one slash.

Atop his bony perch, the Ghoul laughed. This pause allowed all of us to get a good look at him for the first time. Slightly larger than a man, with sinewy muscles visible through a loose and greyish skin, he examined the wound in his side. Wearing the tattered remains of dark-colored breaches and x-shaped leather harness covered in sheathed knives, he looked back down at Brin with those cold, cloudy eyes. They were the same eyes that had stalked me in the warehouse. Yet he seemed different now, more powerful somehow. "You must be the daughter of the Bard. What a savory man your father was. So strong, so charismatic, so stupid, so dead."

Brin tried not to react at this mention of her father. The Shadow had mentioned that the Ghoul knew the person who murdered him. She had prepared herself for this confrontation and was determined not to let this thing uncork her emotions and cloud her vision.

"Come down and fight me you uzkin' pathetic mess. Or do you only prey on the weak and the helpless."

Chapter 11

Again the Ghoul laughed. "Doubtless, I shall call them lunch." The smug thing looked back and forth from Avar to Brin a few times before speaking again. "If it is not to feed me, then why are you here? Doubtless you want to know about your father. Vengeance is so. . .pitiful."

Avar climbed to his feet and went back into a defensive position in front of the children. He could see from Brin's expression that she was starting to lose control of her temper.

"I already know you were one of the ones who killed him, slug. Come down and finish this."

"You do? How surprised would you be to know that I was not even there when he died then? Pathetic girl, I should eat you alive to put an end to your pain and confusion. It could all be over in a few short hours. All the hatred, the loneliness, all of your struggles—gone forever. Just surrender yourself. To my mercy."

Confused by Brin's statement about knowing who killed her father, Avar reverted to bravely standing against their common enemy. "She will never surrender to you, fiend!"

Brin looked back at him, and lowered her weapon. Her jaw clenched as she fought back tears, then turning her gaze back up at the Ghoul she said, "Avar. Free the children."

Avar turned and smashed the cage next to him with his mace sending a shower of bone flying in every direction. Children from the cage screamed excitedly as Avar's mace smashed more of the cage until there was a hole large enough for their small bodies to escape through. Before the cage was empty, Avar moved his mace to the wall of the cage next to it bringing freedom with every blow.

Above the Ghoul looked with horror as his collection of food was being stolen before his eyes. His rage overcame his cowardice, and he leapt down to the floor. The blade in Brin's hands rose to meet the Ghoul's charge, delivering one more wound to his

Wracked

shoulder before his hand swiped Brin. The force of his attack threw Brin across the room like a helpless doll. Her body smashed into the bottom of a stack of cages, smashing the bars. The cages on top toppled over smashing into other cages. This chain reaction caused more than half the cages in the room to fall and burst open. Bone fragments and dust filled the room along with the cheers of excited freed children. A stream of little bodies, some of them carrying others who were wounded or missing limbs, came flooding to the passage where I stood. One of them stopped and turned when he had gone down the tunnel a short distance. Piercing the darkness, I searched the face of the tiny person. At first I thought I saw the curious eyes of the brave boy. As if mocking me, the shadows retreated from his face, and it was another of the boys from outside the walls. Without a word, he turned and ran down the tunnel with the others.

When the sword struck the Ghoul it had again burst with black energy. This time I felt a painful surge at that same moment, and my arms grew cold. My hands so encased in the black and purple energy that I could not make out my own fingers within as the darkness steamed up away from them.

The Ghoul then turned to Avar, who brought his shield up just in time to deflect a knife that had been thrown at him from the Ghoul's harness. The Ghoul drew more knives and leapt at Avar again. Trying to defend the fleeing children, Avar fell under the storm of quick attacks that came from the Ghoul. In a small spray of red, Avar slumped to the floor his legs, face, and arms cut. It had all happened so fast I hadn't had enough time to do anything but stumble into the room.

Those cloudy and dead eyes met mine and the victory which was in his face faded. He backed away from Avar and began to cower in fear.

Chapter 11

"Please! Do not end me! I am pitiful and retched, but I have my uses. Doubtless, I can serve you. Please! I beg you!"

Part of me enjoyed gloating over him. Watching him beg for mercy, that part of me wanted to watch him die slowly. It wanted to make him suffer, not for the suffering he had caused, just simply because I knew I could.

"I had no choice. When I heard you had returned I took your blood to help me fight off the Rotting One. Doubtless, he and the King want to take what is mine. I cannot have nothing! I was promised so much, and I want it! Please!"

My eyes met his again and suddenly I found myself somewhere else.

From across the room, I was looking into the fearful eyes of a man, his unshaven face covered in stubble, his worried face framed in greasy brown hair. His clothes seemed common and dark. The only thing that stood out was the harness of many knives that hung like an x over his chest.

There he was again, just behind the pointy bearded commander, the man with the crown, and the salt and pepper haired man with the burgundy mask. Looking around, I was back in the marble chamber with the vaulted ceiling. At my feet was a bowl full of water, surrounded by candles. The water was clouded with ashes floating within, and in my left hand there was a knife, my hand poised to cut my other exposed arm. I looked over at the man with the knife-filled harness, his face filled with an eagerness mixed with concern.

Wracked

In a flash I saw myself in a different place. The small room seemed to be an audience chamber. At one end of a small table was a chair that was nearly a throne. Seated on that chair was the pointy bearded commander. His macabre armor was intact in all its skull-ridden, tentacle-etched glory. On his chest, the black tabard with red borders now had a red skull on it. Most disturbingly, he was skeletal thin with painful red flesh around his eyes. He reached down and picked up a piece of parchment with an ungloved hand. Three of his fingers had no flesh. Their skeletal forms were as red as the skull painted on his chest. In his other hand rested a scepter topped with a purple gem.

A sickly grey skinned man with a red stain around his mouth came into the room. He silently took the parchment from the hand of the commander. When the grey skinned man turned towards me, I could see the leather harness.

The commander spoke to me without looking in my direction. "Wrack, my boy. As soon as this 'message' is delivered, we will again be at war. Glorious war. The King will be shamed, and I will become king. Baron. Ha! At long last I shall be King."

Unbridled hatred and betrayal overflowed in me, yet my voice responded, "Yes m'lord."

With another flash, there was battle all around me. Men in white and green were fighting shoulder to shoulder with men wearing the red and black. There was no skull on the livery this time. The enemy had forces wearing purple and black with silver trim. Lavish and rich was their armor and their livery., weapons so brilliant that not even combat could dull the reflection of the sun above. Behind their ranks moved a large obsidian pyramid. It floated over the battlefield, creeping moment by moment closer to the front of the battle. It was flanked on either side by a mass of black hooded figures. A tiny glint of silver shined on their chests.

Chapter 11

Fear was filling the army that surrounded me. Men in white and green began to break and run while the pointy bearded commander, alive and unchanged from the killing at the tower, stood fast and commanded his men to do so.

Commotion and violence sped into a complete blur. In this messy smear of light and action, I could not tell what was happening, save that the pyramid was laying waste to the armies before it, shooting silver rays from its tip. Overwhelmed with the vision, I began to panic. I held my breath hoping it would stop, and it did.

Before me lay a pile of dead. Soldiers of every kind lay there, and under them was the living form of the man in the leather harness, blood spilling down into his mouth. At first he tried to move away from it, but then a hunger awoke in him and he began to seek it. He could not get enough of it. Within moments he had removed one of his daggers and was cutting open the corpses on top of him to increase the flow, then he moved to severing entire chunks of flesh and devouring them. I felt him change. I felt him die.

What followed was a series of visions of him committing murders. Some feeling told me that these were contracted killings, not just the random slaughter of people. In each instance he took a trophy from the victim. A piece here, a chunk there. With each trophy consumed, his power became stronger. Over time, the life drained from the color of his skin. His outer shell becoming a grey and waxy reflection of the monster he had become. He stopped keeping up his shabby appearance and let himself go further away from the human he once was. Stringy, greasy hair could not hide the blood stained maw that became his mouth nor could it conceal his dead eyes.

Wracked

"What promise?" I questioned the Ghoul.

His cowering posture dropped slowly and something like a smile began as he stared at me.

"Do you know me?" I urged.

The Ghoul laughed. "Doubtless you know I do. Is this a test?"

I said nothing.

"You are Wrack. Or am I mistaken?"

My face must have betrayed my confusion for his posture changed to one of confidence.

"Have you forgotten? Let me help you remember." Cautiously, he took a few steps toward me, like a cat about to pounce on its prey. He licked his lips, then leapt at me.

Black lightning lashed out at him as he came towards me. Tendrils of the energy streamed out of the main assault and licked at everything around us. The force threw him into the remaining cages. As they broke and fell, a second flood of children ran from the room. A shower of bone fragments and a hanging dust shrouded the Ghoul's escape.

I scanned the room looking for movement. A smell of burnt flesh met my nostrils a moment before I felt a clawed hand tear through my side. I reeled back away from the Ghoul as he produced the small talon charm in his left hand. "Doubtless you are powerless against my new pets. I will eat your heart, and take your power, then even the Baron will kneel to me." Falling to the floor, my eyes met the empty stare of the Ghoul's last meal. The lifeless face of the curious boy from outside the city walls flooded my mind with hatred. A hurricane of rage blew through my soul and I surrendered to it.

Chapter 11

There was a hissing sound as three black spiders with oozing flesh appeared in the room. Unnoticed, the first time I had seen these creatures, the center of those masses of multi jointed legs housed a fanged mouth the size of a dog's. As soon as they appeared, they gracefully jumped in my direction. My hand instinctively reached outward and time seemed to slow as Ukumog which was in Brin's hands flew from her limp grasp into my hand.

As soon as I felt the leather of the handle I felt a completeness that I had not known until that moment. It was as if the lost part of my soul had been fused back into place. It, too, looked as if it had come to life. Suddenly covered in a misty fog of black and purple, only the bright shine of the blue runes pierced the darkness within, and they pulsed with the rushing power through me. We were one.

The blade rose in my hand and in a few short strokes I had cut one of the spidery beasts into a pile of bits. My other hand I raised and suddenly I was holding a shield made entirely of shadow, which deflected the other two beasts. Ukumog and I made short work of them, but it was long enough for the Ghoul to start heading toward the tunnel.

Lunging forward, I grabbed him by the harness that crossed his chest. "Leaving so soon?" Then I tossed him so hard against the back wall of the room that the foundation of the very sewer cracked open.

Blood leaking from his nose and mouth, he leapt up to the chain perch that hung from the ceiling.

"Doubtless you have come to destroy me then! Has your lust for life never been sated?"

"Has yours? These are children you are devouring. Your plague on this world must come to an end."

Wracked

"Plague? Doubtless if this is anyone's, plague it's yours! End yourself!" His limbs slowly responded to his cowardly nature and tried to ease him away from danger.

A evil, heckling laugh grew from a tiny hidden place inside me and grew until it was shaking the walls. From high above, he threw his last remaining daggers at me to cover his escape as he leapt to the tunnel entrance. Each dagger I blocked with ease. As I was taking a breath I realized, I wasn't letting him get away. I was savoring his false sense of success. *His destruction will be so much more delicious if he thinks he has gotten away. That should be far enough.*

I leapt across the entire length of the room and threw Ukumog down the tunnel. It left a tendril of dark energy attached to my arm and zoomed down the tunnel until I could feel it collide with something soft. The blade itself shifted and while I could not see what was happening, I could feel it. A howl of pain and fear fled the tunnel and I began reeling in my catch.

As he came into the light, I saw that the blade had become a barbed hook that was piercing his thigh. It was throbbing with the black and purple energy which was flowing down the tendril down to me. Waves of refreshment and rage were filling me with each pulse.

"Doubtless we have come to your end." I mocked him in a callous and unrelenting voice that I did not recognize as my own, yet I felt it came from deep within my soul.

"Please! Spare us! Doubtless we are pathetic." He cowered before me. "We are just so HUNGRY!" As the Ghoul tried to lash out at me with that final word, I twisted my wrist calmly. Ukumog flew back into my hand tearing off the leg it had been hooked into. The Ghoul's horrible wail filled the chamber, but I didn't hear it. I turned and looked over at Brin who lay on the ground and wondered

Chapter 11

if she were still alive, then his screams invaded my world, and I was angry. It felt like someone inside me pulled my face away from her and looked back down on the Ghoul. I felt no mercy. No remorse. My desire to destroy him was flooding my vision and worse of all, some part of me hungered for his death. It was a hunger like these helpless children hungered for scraps of food at the gates of Yellow Liver or even as the Ghoul hungered for the flesh and blood of the innocent.

The shield vanished from my arm and I placed both hands on the leather wrapped handle of Ukumog. "Who murdered the Bard?" I forced myself to ask as my hands lifted the sword over my head. All he had time to scream before I cut him in half was "The King—"

Ukumog drank deep of the blood and energy that nearly exploded from the two halves of the corpse at my feet. The energy washed over me, filling me with a lust to destroy the Doomed and filling my head with so many images and dreams both that I had seen and hadn't that it was overwhelmingly painful. I felt as if I were losing myself to the horror that I saw in my own thoughts. Using the last tattered part of my willpower, I struggled to throw Ukumog across the room where it buried nearly half its length into the stone wall.

Exhausted, I collapsed to the floor. The energy around me faded and I felt like myself again. One of the blue glowing runes on the side of Ukumog grew brighter and then burst like a soap bubble and the sword grew silent. My lungs gave a breath of relief and I hung my head. Slowly I looked at Avar, who I could sense was still alive, and I watched as his wounds seemed to close rapidly before my very eyes.

Wracked

Life stirred in my robes and Murks jumped out. Scampering across the room, he found the abandoned black talon on the floor. Raising it in his tiny scabby hands he drank from it like man might from a giant tankard of ale. Drops of black blood were squeezed from it and each one seemed to rejuvenate my little hemodan with new life. Feeling his power grow, I pulled the tiny wax mask from my pocket. The black talon cracked and pieces clattered to the floor. The deformed face of the wax mask haunted my thoughts. *Am I the mask or the monster beneath it?*

"Wrack?" Brin's call from behind me ripped me from my thoughts.

Turning, I saw her sitting up. The look on her face told me that she had seen the end of the fight.

The silence in the air was thick with fear and doubt. A single tear falling from her eye she asked, "Who the uzk are you?"

I couldn't look at her as I said, "I don't know."

Made in the USA
Charleston, SC
07 January 2014